About the author

Fiona Dunbar spent much of her childhood secretly drawing cartoon stories in her bedroom, though none of her characters actually came to life. Her first job was drawing storyboards for TV advertisements, after which she became a freelance illustrator. As her head was filling up with stories, she had no choice but to spill them onto the page in the form of picture books, followed by fiction, in the enchanting and critically acclaimed Lulu Baker Trilogy: The Truth Cookie, Cupid Cakes and Chocolate Wishes. Fiona lives in London with her husband and two children. Toonhead is her fourth novel for children.

First published in 2007 by Orchard Press

Orchard Books, 338 Euston Road
London NW1 3BH

Orchard Books Australia
Level 17/207 Kent Street
Sydney, NSW 2000

Text copyright © Fiona Dunbar 2007

2

ISBN 978 1 84616 238 1

Printed and bound in Great Britain by Clays Ltd, St Ives plc

Orchard Books is a division of Hachette Children's Books.

fiona dunbar

Toonhead

ORCHARD BOOKS

In memory of Bernard Stone, 1924-2005

Prologue

I'm sitting on top of the world. Or a pile of poo, depending on how you look at it. How did I get here? Do you really want to know? I've been on a voyage to Hell and back. You know what people mean when they say you're 'gifted'? They mean you have a gift from God. Well let me tell you, there's such a thing as a gift from the devil…

One

I suppose you'll want to know my name. OK, it's Pablo. And before you ask, no I'm not Spanish, not even a teensy bit. My parents are as English as a wet weekend. They called me Pablo because they're artists, you see, so as far as they're concerned, Pablo is just the wickedest name ever, because of Picasso, right? You know, the dead famous, supposedly biggest mega-genius artist ever in the entire history of the universe? I know this all off by heart, (you can guess why): he painted every day of his life for ninety-two years, never stopped painting apparently even in his sleep, changed the way everybody in the whole world looked at things for ever after, and invented the theory of relativity. No, I made that last bit up. Oh, and all the women he ever met fell madly in love with him and he got to be really horrible to them, 'cause they wouldn't leave him alone, right, and they'd be banging on the door of his studio, whole crowds of them going, 'Pablo, Pablo, we love you, we love you', and all that sicky stuff. So he'd raise one hand and click his fingers, right, not saying a word, cool as a cucumber, and these fierce dogs would come out, whoosh, and bite their bums and chase them all away. Here I go again, making stuff up. I do that.

Anyway, he's the one they named me after. Boy, am I a disappointment to them! Even their clothes look disappointed. Because I *am* no Pablo Picasso, and I won't ever be. Ha! Sounds ridiculous, right? I'm *twelve*, for Pete's sake! But it's true: they want me to be brilliant at art, totally in love with art, making art, talking art, art, art, art all the time just like they do, and I don't. I just don't.

I remember back when I was four and for a minute there, they thought they had me sorted out. Because they figured, well hey, maybe Pablo's just suffering from creative block. That's it! Pablo's a brilliant artist really, it's just that he's stuck for ideas at the moment! So there I was, sitting up in bed one morning, and Mum said, 'Somewhere at the base of your brain, Pablo dear, there's a juice box that's blocked.'

And Dad, getting into the metaphor, doing the 'let's explain difficult stuff to our four year old' thing, said, 'Yes, son. That little foil bit that covers the hole where the straw goes? Well that bit is probably still closed, and nothing's getting through the straw.' The genius juice was collecting in the box and had nowhere to go. Hey Presto!

8

So what did Mum do? Next day, she whizzed me off to see some friend of Aunt Dot's; Katinka Tinkar, holistic juice box un-blocker. Me, I just screamed 'til I was blue in the face, I wasn't having any of it. Well, wouldn't you? I mean, they might have been a bit more careful with their metaphors. I was convinced that Katinka Tinkar would be coming at me with a giant pointy-ended straw, trying to make holes in me. 'Specially as she described herself as a *holistic* healer. I mean, come on! Adults are so dumb sometimes.

Eventually I calmed down. Actually, it was easy to calm down in Katinka Tinkar's flat, as it was all lush and green, just crammed with plants. So first thing I think is, wicked! Tarzan! Now here I've got to explain something. If my mum and dad had their way, I wouldn't ever have heard of Tarzan. It's not the sort of thing that comes up in our house. You wouldn't have Mum and Dad going, 'Shall we take a two-hour tube and train ride to Croydon to hear someone we slightly know give a talk on colour theory?' – 'No, I hear there's a fab movie about this kid that grows up in the jungle with the apes, and it's got loads of adventure and Pablo'll think it's just fantastic!' Not in a million years! That's just not the sort of thing we *do*; it's what other families do. Oh, I get to see films sometimes. I saw one about Beauty and the Beast once, but it was in black and white and in French with not very good special effects. It gave me nightmares.

Anyway, Tarzan. The way I knew about Tarzan, I should say, was from my mates in nursery school (obviously, we don't have a telly in our house). Eventually the Tarzan game came to an end and instead I had to lie down while Katinka Tinkar pressed bits of me and wiggled my toes. Sounds daft, but I seem to remember being dead calm so I must not have minded it.

So, after I'd been to her a few times, Mum, Dad and Dot decided they should, you know, check the results. They brought me to my room, where there were paper, paint, clay, the works. All laid on like I was Lord of the Manor arriving for dinner. I obediently sat down, and stared blankly at all the stuff. I looked up at Dad. 'Help me!' said a tiny voice inside.

He didn't hear. 'Just do anything you like, Pablo,' he said, spreading his hands. 'Anything at all!'

I looked at Mum. She just beamed at me eagerly.

Aunt Dot grinned her brown-toothed grin. 'Let your mind fly free as a bird in the sky,' she said, or some such twaddle.

Then the door was closed and I was alone. I stared at the great expanse of plain white cartridge paper, the grey lump of clay, the brushes and pots.

'Help me!'

Well, I did use my imagination, but they weren't very pleased. That's putting it mildly. I thought I'd done pretty well, actually, but apparently they didn't see it that

10

way. I mean, if you were being Tarzan, and there was no jungle, well, you'd *imagine* it, wouldn't you? So if there was like, something dangling from the ceiling, then that's just fantastic, because you could pretend it was one of those ropey things that he uses to swing from one tree to another. I had this mobile, you see – no, not a phone, but one of those dangly-jangly things. It hung pretty low, and well, after I'd made a snake with the clay I got a bit bored – they did leave me alone in there for ages – so I got into my Tarzan game.

Crash! Down I came, the mobile as well, and half the ceiling with it.

Mum rushed in. 'Pablo dear, what happened?'

Then Dad and Aunt Dot. Not worried about me like Mum, not checking me for broken bones or anything. Aunt Dot barely glanced at me, and instead was straight away searching the room for evidence of creative genius; all she and Dad seemed to care about was (a) why hadn't I been making art, and (b) how dare I destroy art, because that's what the mobile was, art. That's right, you understood correctly, I was four years old and I had a valuable piece of art in my bedroom. Is that weird, or what?! Not any of those wicked things other boys had – you know, Action Men and fire trucks that go *WEEYOWEEYOW!* – no they'd have no truck with that, ha ha. Just a few wooden things, some serious books I couldn't read, and a mobile that was a real work of art. And here I was, their worst nightmare: I didn't just dislike art, I must have hated it, because I killed it.

They finally had to admit that the genius juice must have skipped a generation.

My juice box was empty.

Two

Don't you just love cartoons? I think they're the business, I could watch them all day long. Anything's possible in cartoons, isn't it? People get bashed and crashed and blown to bits, and then they just pick themselves up, shake it off and go on their way, all new again like nothing ever happened to them. Or they fly off the edge of a cliff and just hang there until they look down and *that's* when they start to fall. It happens time and time and time again. You think, well, why don't they learn that next time, if they don't look down, they'll be OK? Just keep on going, don't look down, and pretty soon you'll be on the other side of the canyon or whatever. Simple! If I were a cartoon, that's what I would do.

Yeah, I know you're thinking, what's he on about, he doesn't even have a TV, how does he know all this stuff? I'd like to say I spent a lot of time in my friends' houses and watched them there, but – ooh, no, they were onto that one, my mum and dad. They spotted that little shack wa-a-ay off in the distance and said, 'No way, n'uh-uh, we're not stopping here, we're keeping on going 'til we're in the Almighty Kingdom of Dead Brainy Stuff and Trash-Free Streets.' 'Cause that's what cartoons are, they're trash. They pollute your mind and make you stupid. They'll make me stupid, I expect. Eventually I'll be dumb enough to sit there and go, 'Hey, I needn't worry if I get squashed by a steam-roller, 'cause all that will happen is I'll be flat for a few seconds, and then I'll be all right, and you know what, that sounds fun, I think I'll go and try it right now.'

So no, I don't get to hang out at my mates' houses, and they don't hang out at mine. Actually I'd be embarrassed to have mates round to my place. For one thing, there's not much space; the rooms in our house get smaller year by year, as more and more stuff piles up around the edges. One day there won't be any space left for us, and instead you'll have a great solid mass that you could slice through the middle and see the layers that you could date like rings in a tree-trunk. 'Ah yes, that was Wenda Hobbs' crushed crockery phase: 1987-88; and look, here's Humphrey Hobbs' bodily fluids phase: 1998-99.' The trouble is, not an awful lot of it gets sold. Even the garden shed's been taken over – it's where Dad makes metal sculptures that I don't understand. He explained them to me once, but it was all to do with maths and physics and made no sense to me at all.

Then there's the smell. You walk in the front door and it hits you right away: turpentine. Dad paints in the living room, or rather we live in the painting room. Which is also the dining room, so everything you eat tastes of turpentine, which is a bit like listening to your favourite tune inside the engine room of a gigantic ship. And the bathroom! The bathroom was once a darkroom, which is what people used for developing photographs before computers. It's not used as a darkroom any more, but you'd never know it. It still has black curtains and a red light bulb, great big dusty old brown jars of chemicals, and an 'enlarger', a monster steel thing that looks like an instrument of torture, which looms over you when you're on the toilet. Dad was convinced that one day he'd get back to photography – 'but not any of that digital nonsense' – so he wouldn't get rid of the stuff.

More recently he was going through his black line phase; just painting straight black lines on white backgrounds. This was around the time Mum got into her dead people phase, and I think it was getting her down. For six months she was working on the same piece, one and a half by two metres, which she was covering with tiny zip-lock bags containing dead peoples' hair and toenail clippings. And I *mean* dead; she went to the morgue regularly to collect them. And under each bag she'd write the person's name and the cause of death. All that time at the morgue was doing her head in, I think.

Imagine me bringing my mates home to all that! I'd be all the time going, 'Oh, don't mind that, it's just my mum's collection of bits of dead people; no, the bathroom really isn't a torture chamber; yes, I know the stew tastes of turpentine, but you'll just have to take my word for it that there isn't any actually in it.'

Now, if you grew up in a home with say, a pet aardvark, you wouldn't know at first that there was anything unusual about it. It's only when you go to other people's homes and they don't have aardvarks, and you might say, 'Have you got an aardvark?' And they'd look at you like you were mad, that you'd realise that the vast majority of homes are aardvark-free zones.

I'm telling you this just so as you'll have some idea of what it felt like, the day I got to see the inside of Donald's house. It was clean! It was tidy! It didn't smell of turpentine!

And you want to know how many tellies they've got at his place? Five. *Five.* Donald's dad, you see, he's American, he's this big cheese in Cable TV. His whole life is TV. He gets up in the morning and bang, it's in his face and it's news, weather, stock-market reports, news, sport, more news. He's got a telly in the car and a telly in the toilet, electronically programmed to pump up the volume when he flushes in case he misses anything. He wears a telly on his wrist and walks along the street with his arm out in front of him like some martial arts freak.

He's got a device that he wears in bed that feeds telly into his dreams…I'm making stuff up again, you probably guessed that. I can't help it. Anyway, you get the idea: TV is his work and his play and he never switches off.

It happened when Mum and Dad were staying overnight in Manchester for some big exhibition. Normally they'd arrange for me to stay with Aunt Dot, but she was away too so, well, even *my* parents have to let me stay with someone else in a situation like that. And lucky for me, that someone was Donald and his family. Cornelius, his brother, is like, twenty-one or something, and he gets off work early so he stays with Donald 'til their mum and dad come home from work. So there I was, being shown into this living room and there in front of me was just the most gee-i-normous telly I'd ever seen. Donald wagged the remote at it and it flicked into life, all bursting with colour and stereophonic sound. I must have looked daft, 'cause after a bit I noticed him smirking at me. He knew this was a first for me, and he was enjoying getting a reaction.

'Cool, huh?'

'It's…yeah!'

Cornelius came in with a massive bowl of crisps and some cans of cola and flopped onto the couch. I watched mesmerised as a tall grey creature with long ears and goofy teeth appeared on the screen.

Another – apparently human – creature with a bald head chased the long-eared thing into a hole in the ground, then began firing into the hole, *blam blam*! with his rifle. He was still doing this when long-ears ambled over to his side, produced a carrot and took a bite.

'What's up, doc?' said Cornelius and long-ears, at exactly the same time.

'How'd he know he'd say that?' I said to Donald.

He let out a squeak of laughter and he and Cornelius glanced at each other.

'He's never seen telly before,' Donald explained.

'Give over,' said Cornelius, 'you're pulling my chain.'

'No, really,' insisted Donald. 'Right, Pabs?'

I was still glued to the screen. 'Wha'?'

'You've never watched telly before.'

I nodded. ''S'right.'

Cornelius sat up. 'You mean you *really* don't know who Bugs Bunny is?'

'That's his name?'

Well, you'd have thought I'd said I'd never heard of Christmas. Twenty questions right there.

'Blimey,' said Cornelius at last. 'Not much of a chillout scene round your gaff, is there?'

'Er…no.'

He raised one eyebrow in mock-seriousness.

'*Interrresting*…pull up a seat, have a crisp or five. Relax, you're standing there like a tent-pole!'

I slid into the nearest seat. 'Well, I s'pose I could, just for a while…'

Cornelius elbowed Donald and winked. 'We gotta get this boy a *hed-u-cation!*'

*   *   *

Coming home after school the next day, I realised just how messy and cluttered our own house was. Mum and Dad hadn't been back long, and Mum was faffing about with some bags of shopping that were spilling onto the table and mingling with the paintbrushes and dirty rags. I went to the fridge, and what should be staring me in the face but a bag of baby carrots! I grabbed the bag and munched a couple.

'Rice!' groaned Mum. 'I forgot the bloomin' rice! Back in a minute.'

I smacked my lips as I finished my carrot. Before I knew it, I was Bugs burrowing into the sofa. I was Bugs up on the chair, I was Bugs under it. I was Elmer chasing Bugs, I was Elmer shooting with the long paintbrushes. *'Pcchhoow! Pcchhoow!'*

'Pablo, what on earth are you doing?' said Mum, back from the shop with a pack of rice in her hand.

'Uh, nothing!' I shrugged. I grabbed the carrots and shot up to my room. There, I found myself a pristine pencil and drawing pad, sadly collecting dust on a shelf.

How did he look, now? A bunny rabbit. Not like any bunny rabbit you ever saw, though! I scrunched up my eyes, then tried to draw what came into my head. It was rubbish. I tore it up and started again.

That was pretty useless, too; there were teeth and there were ears, there were long arms and legs, but it looked nothing like him. I stood there, munching carrots. I shut my eyes again. *Pesky wabbit! I know you's in there somewhere!* Carrots are supposed to help you see in the dark, aren't they? I tore off the page and tried again, and again. I filled page after page with my tries. Then I heard Dad mounting the stairs, and in no time he was outside my door.

'Yuh, hi!' I yelled, as I frantically shoved the last piece of paper under the bed. I almost burst into hysterics. Here I was, finally showing some interest in drawing, which was what they wanted all along, and what was I doing? *Hiding* what I'd done!

Three

I suppose it's meant to be a Good Thing that our family sits down and talks at dinnertime. You know, they say that, don't they? I can't help thinking, though, that other families have more fun over dinner. Here's what it's like in our household:

Me: Mum, I'm invited to a football party next Saturday. I really want to go.

Mum: No dear, that's the day we're going to that exhibition I told you about, remember?

Me: Oh no! Not that guy who does the piles of cardboard boxes! Oh, *Mum!*

Dad: *(severely)* At least it will engage your brain, young man; you play football with your friends at school all the time. And you know how we feel about parties. Such rampant displays of consumerism only serve to engender a culture of acquisitiveness in the younger generation. *(Translation: parties just teach kids to want too many presents. I bet you're wondering what they do for my birthdays. You don't want to go there, believe me.)*

Of course, I knew this was what they'd say, and in fact there was no football party. I just asked, because then I could act all hurt and disappointed, and make them feel guilty, which would make them more likely to say yes to my next question. I waited a bit before asking it. I hunched my shoulders forward, forming the most tragic expression on my phizog as I could muster. I heaved a sigh, and said, 'I suppose you won't want me to do chess club, either.'

Dad looked up. 'Chess club?'

'Yeah, Donald's brother was telling me about it on the way home; he's going to be running it. Donald's gonna do it. But – *sigh!* – I suppose…'

'There are games, and there are games, Pablo,' interrupted Dad. 'And chess, I think, is an excellent idea. Who knows? Perhaps it might even exercise that tiny creative impulse that's buried in there somewhere,' he added sarcastically, prodding my head.

I felt a little flip of glee inside. 'So I can do it?'

Dad nodded. 'All right. I assume there'll be a consent form?'

Yippee! How do you like that, they actually fell for it! Tuesday afternoons, and I'd be off to the House of Tellies for two whole hours of pure perfect uninterrupted silliness. I did feel a bit bad, but I told myself that if we ever got found out, Cornelius would be the one in the

22

deepest do-do's. I almost didn't agree to it myself, 'cause I was worried about being found out. But then I thought, well, since Mum and Dad never talk to the other parents, that wasn't very likely anyway. Mum's just too wrapped up in her work, and Dad…well, Dad reminds me of those fossilised fish you get in museums, closed off from the world in a glass case, captured forever in a permanent expression of disappointment. It's his dried-fishness, that's the reason he's not pally with anyone. He might grin, but like a fish; it doesn't involve his eyes.

* * *

'How was chess?'

I was standing in the doorway, Cornelius's 4x4 purring behind me as it trailed into the darkness. I looked at Mum's shoes; I didn't want her to see my eyes, because I couldn't help thinking she'd be able to see the cartoons reflected there. My face burned. *Stop it, stop it!*

'Oh, great! Er…better do my homework now!' I said, and bolted upstairs.

I shoved some heavy books up against the door, pulled out the drawing stuff and went to it, right there on the floor. The floor just felt like the right place for it somehow. The desk was the place for homework, but down there on my belly among the dust balls and biscuit crumbs, I was as happy as a puppy in the park. An hour went by in five minutes.

* * *

After supper, during which Aunt Dot stopped by and there were yet more questions about my chess game, I was off to my room again.

'Aren't you going to stay and listen to the Hamster Concerto with us?' asked Aunt Dot.

'The what?'

'The Hamster Concerto,' repeated Dad. 'It's an entire concerto played on hamsters and guinea pigs. It's highly original.'

'Sounds horribly cruel to me.'

Dad looked pained. 'Art is suffering, suffering is art, Pablo.'

'Er…I think I'll go and do my homework.'

'I thought you'd finished it,' said Mum.

'Well, I'm going to do some extra.'

'Good boy, excellent,' said Dad. 'He has a mind at least, Wenda. All is not quite lost.'

I've always spent a lot of time alone in my room, largely because (a) I don't get to hang out with my mates, and (b) I don't want to sit in a room stinking of turpentine listening to Hamster Concertos. I used to get pretty bored – you can tell things are bad when you're reduced to playing with Joey Sock-Face and Ollie Underpants – but now I had all these images racing before me, and it was *whoosh!* get it down before it fades. It was an explosion! What started with a wobbly bunny was now this incredible cast of characters coming to life on the page. It was like hurtling down a mountainside, I couldn't stop and I was living it and everything else was just a blur as I whizzed by. It was like space dust in my head. I'd found my juice box, and it was overflowing.

I was dead worried that first night, though. Not about being found out, but because I didn't sleep a wink. My head was buzzing with Ed, Edd and Eddy and Tom and Jerry and Richie Roach and Daffy Duck. I drifted into a half-sleep, but then a cute little mouse came and propped up my eyelids with matches, and over there was a cowardly dog howling at the moon, and over here was a boy in big glasses inventing other cartoon characters in his laboratory: and here's another one, *voom!* and here's another one, *voom!* and I'm trying to tell them all, 'theh-the-theh-the-that's all folks!' but each time the closing credits come up, they're pushed away by Yosemite Sam or Wily Coyote.

Phew!

I had the mother of all headaches in the morning, and like I said, I was dead worried. I was worried that I might throw my arms around Mum and go, 'Take me to the doctor, now! I've been a bad boy, I watched telly for two whole hours, and you were right all along – I've given myself *permanent brain damage*. Help me!'

I didn't, of course. Donald said it's like trying anything for the first time, like cycling a long way, or eating Indian food; not too comfortable first time around. Makes sense, I suppose. There was my brain, starved of

25

anything that wasn't wholegrain and dry and crunchy for twelve years, then all of a sudden *wham!* chocolate fudge sundae, bellyache in the head.

Which just goes to show, lentils may be good for you, but we all need a bit of chocolate now and then.

Four

I bet Picasso liked cartoons. I've been reading this book about him, and I reckon he probably watched them, you know. He certainly did them; he did cartoons of his friends all the time. They'd sit around in cafes for hours and his mates would say, 'Go on, Pabs, draw that fat lady over there,' and he'd do it and it'd be brilliant and they'd all just crack up. He did strip cartoons, too, with minotaurs and men on horses and stuff. For once I'm not making it up; he really did.

I can't imagine Mum or Dad ever having that much fun. Or Aunt Dot for that matter. They work and work, but do any of them ever get really *excited* about it, the way I am when I draw? I don't see it. I mean, when I'm drawing I'm more '*me*' than I've ever been in my life. Is that allowed?

How can I explain? OK, take Richie Roach, for instance. You ever seen that show? I really like Richie. He's a cockroach, and he lives at Hope Springs Roach

Motel in Under-the-Sinksville, N.J. Ha! ha! Right there, you can see why I identify with him, right? He's a dreamer and a storyteller, spends his entire life trying to escape into the great wide world, but whenever he gets away it all goes pear-shaped and he always winds up right back where he started. His arch-enemy is the deeply annoying superhero cockroach, Slomo Flash, who thinks he's the cat's pyjamas and is always 'rescuing' Richie, and getting all the glory back at the Motel among the girl cockroaches, who go, 'Slomo, Slomo, we love you!' and poor old Richie can't really say anything, 'cause the sad truth is, Slomo's usually got him out of some big scrape. Richie also has to be dead careful to steer well clear of Gladiator, the tin-opening cat, and Sergeant Salami, the sausage guard-dog. But the big threat to the whole of Under-the-Sinksville is when the Acme Pest Control van comes round, and then they have to get down into their bunker PDQ, or risk being fumigated to death.

Anyway, it was when I was drawing Richie that I got into doing stories. You know, I'd kind of got the hang of drawing him, so I decided it was time for a bit of action. It happened on a Sunday; Aunt Dot was round for lunch. You might have gathered by now that Aunt Dot practically lives at our place; she's Mum's sister, and her house is across the road. Did I tell you *she's* an artist as well? Yeah, and all she ever paints is dots. Big dots, little dots, candy-coloured dots, sludgy browny dots. Dots on the ceiling, dots on the couch, plastic dots, wooden dots, and so on and on with the endless dots. She says it's nothing to do with her name, and gets really annoyed if anyone makes a wise-crack about her painting herself or something. And you don't want to get Aunt Dot annoyed, believe me. She's loud enough as it is, and I don't mean just noise-wise; you should *see* the way she dresses. She only ever wears green, the brighter the better, and puts lime green on her eyelids. Her teeth on the other hand are a deep, dark brown, and match the rich walnut wood of the pipe she smokes.

Well, we had just finished lunch, and Aunt Dot was arguing with Dad about Lines v. Dots, you know, like you do of a Sunday afternoon. You can imagine how much fun I get on weekends. Ha!

'As I always say,' said Aunt Dot, lighting her pipe (Aunt Dot always says 'as I always say…')

'As I always say, we live in a dot-com world, so what could be a more important thing to paint than the dot?'

'Pah!' sniffed Dad. 'What utter rot. It's the *line* that says the most about the world. A line can go on to infinity; it says, where to next? People talk about *lines* of communication. They say, 'what *line* of business are you in?' and 'are you on*line*?' The whole point is, lines mean connections, and where would we be without connections? Nowhere, just sitting still like a stupid dot.'

'Oh, now Humphrey…' Mum began meekly as she stacked the plates. Nobody took any notice.

'Aha!' exclaimed Aunt Dot, jabbing the air with her pipe like she was aiming a dart. 'That's the whole point! That's what people say, isn't it? And you've just said it yourself: "the whole *point*".'

'I think what Humphrey meant was—' Mum warbled.

'A point is a dot, is it not?' went on Aunt Dot, oblivious. 'As I always say, one must have a point in life. One starts out as a mere dot, one lives and dies, ashes to ashes, and then, dot dot dot…what comes next? No one knows.'

It was at this moment that I burst out laughing. This is something that is literally frowned upon in our household. All three faces frowned upon me.

'Sorry,' I said.

Aunt Dot went all fiery-eyed in a squinty, lime-greeny sort of way. 'Am I to take it, Pablo, that the principles on which I have based a lifetime's work…that these are something which you find…*funny?*'

Actually, what I'd been thinking was how much at that moment she looked like Sergeant Salami, the sausage guard-dog. 'No, really Aunty, I don't…' I attempted, before I was convulsed again.

Aunt Dot turned to Dad. 'So much for your lines of communication, Humphrey. He's your only son, and I see no sign that he's learnt a single thing from either of you. Young people today must have a *point* in life, as I always say—'

'Oh shut up, Dot,' snapped Dad. 'What would *you* know about bringing up children, you've never even—'

'Humphrey!' gasped Mum, turning bright red.

Aunt Dot was positively sizzling, and I could swear her shirt turned a brighter shade of green. 'Well Humphrey, I may never have been fortunate enough to have children of my own, but it's just as well I'm around to knock young Pablo here into shape!'

That really wound Dad up. Luckily, they were so busy arguing, and Mum was burying herself in the washing-up, nobody noticed me slope off to my room.

I got down on the floor and lost myself in doodles. It's how I get the ideas going; doodles and words. It won't surprise you to learn that the words I wrote were *Mad* and *Sad*. Mad, that's Dot. And Sad, that's Mum. I felt sorry for her; I really wished she'd get away from that morgue, it was slowly turning her into a zombie. 'Hey everybody, meet my un-dead Mum!' Oh, whatever happened to make my family so weird?

It's a *Mystery*. Dot dot dot.

Richie and the Mystery Dots.

Hmm, not a bad title. Let's see now: Richie's escaped Under-the-Sinksville, and he's got as far as the kitchen table when he notices these dots on the floor, looking like cockroach footprints. So he follows the dots, all the way up the table leg, and there it is. A big bowl of...what? Salsa, that's it. Cockroaches love salsa, I decided. The spicier the better. So there they are, having a salsa party, diving in and tortilla-surfing and singing, 'la cucaracha, la cucaracha, da -na nanna nanna na!' and Richie, well he just can't help himself. Or rather he does help himself; this is too good a chance to be missed and in he goes. And they're all having so much fun, filling their bellies and getting all fired up with chilli-hotness, they don't notice Gladiator the cat creeping up. Next thing, Gladiator's got Richie dangling from the end of his claw, while the others all scarper fast as you like. Gladiator licks his lips, then opens wide and he's lowering Richie into his mouth, and poor Richie's hanging there, saying his prayers when…

Suddenly he has a brilliant idea. So he goes, 'STOP!' and Gladiator stops, and Richie says, 'There's something much tastier than me, and I know where to get it.' He points to the now empty salsa bowl and says, 'It's the best stuff in the world, better than a dish of cream, makes you feel like a million dollars. And there's another jar of it in the cupboard.' Gladiator, who can open jars as well as tins, is curious so he shoves Richie into his collar and follows his instructions 'til he finds the other jar. Nice close-up here of the label which reads 'Extra-Hot Jalapeño Peppers!' (Gladiator can't read, of course.) And Richie goes, 'You gotta swallow the whole lot in one go, to get the best out of it,' and Gladiator, being dumb, goes for it. Cue scenes of cat turning red, then purple, hitting the ceiling and all that kind of stuff, during which Richie manages to wriggle free and scuttle off. He makes it to the window ledge and he's *this* close to freedom, he can see the birdies and the butterflies and the lambikins frolicking in the distant green fields when *whoosh!* there's Slomo Flash whisking him off back to Under-The-Sinksville, and there's all the girlies going, 'Oh Slomo, you made it, you fought off the big, bad cat, you're our hero!'

Cue fed up Richie, The End.

Five

So what's so brill about that? I hear you ask. And you'd have a point; it's not bad as cartoon stories go, but it's hardly earth-shattering stuff. That's what I thought too, so as usual I brought it to school for Donald (who was collecting my drawings so my parents wouldn't discover the evidence) and I went on to my next idea. But wait...

Picture the scene: it's next Tuesday and I'm sprawled across the enormous black leather sofa at Donald's. You don't sit on that sofa, you sprawl; like losing yourself in a giant's glove, it is. Donald's dog is sprawling, too; this is a very doggy, leathery sort of house but in a spick-and-span, shiny chrome mod cons, American kind of way, not the smelly, hairy, worn-out English way. And Cornelius is sprawling, in jeans wide as an elephant's backside, jeans so lazy that they only remember to separate into legs when they get to the knee section, and can't be bothered to cover up

Cornelius' underwear. And he's got his black-and-red T-shirt on, the one I like with the zombie-skull with a dagger in its eye. Cornelius says he'll get me one for my birthday – ha! Can you imagine?

So there we are, crunching on corn chips, and we've just got through the bit where we sing along to this completely puke-making CD ad they've shown ten zillion times, only of course we do a very rude version. Richie Roach comes on. It starts out with the woman's legs standing by the sink (you do see humans sometimes in Richie Roach, but like in Tom and Jerry, only from the waist-down). So there she is, and then she opens the cupboard door, the door to Under-the-Sinksville. Somebody calls her and she yells back, 'Just a minute!' and she's rummaging around trying to find something. Then she's called again, and this time she slams the door and goes off. But the door rebounds behind her, and there it is, open. Now we see Richie, and he's thrilled to bits and off he goes, scuttle scuttle, fast as his little legs will carry him. Then he sees these dots on the floor, and I think to myself, *hang on!* Richie's following the dots, and they're red, and they look like cockroach footprints. My hair starts tingling, and I cough on my corn chips. Cornelius looks over, *'You all right, mate?'* and pats me on the back.

Now Richie's up on the table, and *there's the bowl of salsa!*

35

I abandon my sprawl, and try to sit up, accidentally kicking the dog in the process. This makes me cough some more, and Cornelius goes, 'You want some water?' and I croak: *'IT'S THE SALSA!'*

Cornelius inspects me through one eye. 'We haven't got any salsa.'

I grab his arm, lunging forward on my knees, and yell, 'No, look!' as I point to the screen, and there's all the roaches singing and dancing, going, *'La cucaracha, la cucaracha, da -na nanna nanna na!'*

And now the dog woofs and starts circling on the couch, and all three of us career this way and that, losing ourselves in the folds of leather as we attempt to get upright, but the sofa is winning and emitting farts of satisfaction. Donald, who was in the next room doing his homework, comes in to find out what all the fuss is about.

'THAT'S *MY* SALSA!' I try to explain. 'Whathappens nextisGladiatorcomesalongandgetsholdofRichie– *aaargh! There he is*! OK,nextthingisRichietalkshimoutof eatinghim—'

'OK, so you've seen this one before,' drawls Cornelius, hoiking himself back onto the sofa so he can resume his sprawl.

'It's never been on before, it's a brand new series!' I screech.

Donald looks at me, looks at the TV set, and his jaw drops. 'Oh, my…' Then he disappears.

Now Gladiator's got Richie dangling from his claw, and I say, 'I don't believe this, this is *exactly*...now he's going to...oh boy, this is *incredible!*' And so it goes on, the whole show, just as I predicted it.

By the time Richie was back at the Hope Springs Roach Motel, and the girlie roaches were going, 'Slomo, Slomo,' etc. Donald had returned with my drawings. Cornelius finally understood what I was so excited about, but even so, he wasn't convinced.

'OK, I know you *think* you've never seen it before, but you must of. It's a cartoon! They repeat them all the time! Did they *say* it was a brand new series?'

'Well, no, but—'

'There you are then. You saw it once, but you don't remember. That's all!'

That's all folks. Cornelius had a point, and Donald seemed to think it was the most logical explanation, too.

I paused, staring at my drawings. 'Well,' I said at last. 'There's only one way to find out...'

Six

The way to find out, of course, would be to try to predict something that happened in real life. But we got stuck in a mega traffic jam on the way home, and by the time I'd got back, had dinner and done my homework (of which I had an extra double dose) I was good for nothing. I fell asleep on my pencil and pad, and woke up with drool on the paper and a whacking great pencil-shaped dent in my face.

So I gave up and went to bed, but then I couldn't sleep. The duvet slid to the floor. Bleary-eyed, I yanked it up and tried to fling the four sides north, south, east, and west, except the southern bit landed in the west leaving my feet sticking out the bottom. This not sleeping business was becoming a bad habit. But I kept on thinking about Richie Roach, that think bubble just wouldn't go away. *How* did I do it? Was it really something I'd already seen? I couldn't believe that. Coincidence? Impossible. So did this really mean I could predict things that happened in real life? Me, who never even managed to wear my anorak on the right day? Perhaps I could only see into the future through my drawings?

This was hopeless. I switched on the light and got out of bed. I'll have another go, I decided: draw tomorrow and see if I'm right. Then I'll know. Tomorrow was Wednesday: well, I knew I'd be going to school, it didn't take a clairvoyant to work that one out. Maths, I think, then History…lunch…oh no, it was all so *predictable!* I decided to stop thinking about tomorrow and try to just draw whatever came into my head. What came into my head was a big man with a beard, wearing a jacket with lots of pockets, eating cornflakes. Then I drew him in a playground; he went down a slide, but got stuck halfway. The playground was very rocky, not like a normal playground at all. The man came unstuck and got off the slide, then went and picked up a rock, which wasn't a rock at all but a human skull. I threw the pencil down. A *skull!* Oh no, this was getting too spooky now! And it was a complete load of old tosh. I shoved it all away, got into bed, and eventually, exhausted, fell asleep.

* * *

Donald came and got my drawing from me as we were packing up for morning break. 'Come on then, let's take a look!' he said eagerly.

I flipped it over to him. 'Don't get excited. It's a load of old drivel.'

Donald opened up the drawing and squinted as he tried to make some sense of it.

'Look, just put it away, will you?' I said, embarassed.

'Come on, let's go.'

'All right, all right!' said Donald, folding it up. 'By the way, I looked up 'clairvoyant' in my encyclopedia last night.'

Oh yeah?' I said, stifling a yawn.

'Did you know it's French for 'seeing clearly'?

'No.'

'Yeah, I thought that was interesting. But I couldn't find anything about drawings. Lots of stuff about tea leaves, palm-reading, tarot cards…no drawings.'

I shrugged. 'Mmm, well…'

'Here, maybe you can do that other stuff too! Ever tried reading tea leaves?'

'We only have tea bags in our house.'

'You look at tea leaves, right,' Donald went on, 'and you see a shape, then you have to figure out what the shape means. Same thing with tarot cards; the pictures on them could tell more than one story. You have to know how to read the signs.'

'I can't do anything like that. I dunno, maybe Cornelius is right, I must've remembered it. I just don't remember remembering it…'

Just then, Miss Tite clapped her hands loudly for attention. 'I've just been told that you are to go to the lecture room after break, instead of coming back here.

40

We weren't sure he'd be able to make it, but I'm pleased to inform you that archaeologist, Dr Henderson Spoon, is scheduled to give a talk in place of the usual history lesson…' Her voice was soon drowned out by the cheers. Not because anyone was particularly excited about Dr Henderson Spoon, but just because going to a talk, any talk, was less like work than being in the classroom.

The moment he walked in, I recognised him. There he was, the man from my drawing. The man in the playground – only not in the playground. I was covered in goose bumps, and my mind was running in all different directions at once. I peered around the auditorium and found Donald, who made saucer-eyes at me; he could see it too. I turned back and stared at Dr Henderson Spoon, archaeologist, complete with big, bushy beard and his coat of many pockets… archaeologist, of course! He digs up bones for a living; that explained the rocks…even the skull! Oh wow.

But why had I seen him in a playground eating cornflakes? I listened for clues.

'It is not uncommon for an archaeologist to spend his or her entire life looking for something and never finding it…' he said.

Good grief, I thought, that's Mum and Dad!'

'…However, make no mistake, there is no such thing as an archaeological dig that's a waste of time. Not everyone can uncover Tutankhamun's tomb, but every bit of land is a treasure trove, something we can all learn from. Now I've brought along some slides…'

Slides. Bing! That's it…that's why I drew a playground. OK, wrong kind of slide, but I was picking up something. My heart pounded and my face went all hot the way it does if I have to recite a poem in class; the excitement of wondering what would come next was almost more than I could take. And suddenly it all made sense to me: clairvoyance, like Donald said, is all about knowing how to read the *signs*. There were signs right there in my strip cartoon of Dr Henderson Spoon, but at the time I drew it they didn't make any sense to me. Which is hardly surprising; who ever used old-fashioned slides any more? OK: in my drawings the man had got stuck in the slide. Perhaps that meant that the slide projector would get stuck…

Sure enough, about halfway through the slide show, the machine packed up. Incredible. Last of all, we were allowed to go up and handle, yes, you guessed it, a Paleolithic skull. I was in a daze, but all I could think of was cornflakes. Then I got it; there *were* no cornflakes, it was just another sign that I didn't read quite right. I'd put them in because I was making an association with the word 'spoon'.

So it was official: Pablo Hobbs was indeed a true clairvoyant. I didn't know whether to be thrilled or freaked out by it, but one thing I knew for sure; things were going to get very interesting from now on…

Seven

I needed some quiet time by myself to think.

The rank, soggy smell that belongs only to school toilets squelched its way through my senses as I sat there, wondering just how far into the future I could see. Beyond tomorrow and the next day, perhaps...right into next year, even?

'Psst! Pabs!' Donald's voice echoed from outside the cubicle.

Maybe I could even see things *years* ahead! Hey, I might even be able to predict my GCSE results...or what kind of job I would get! Would I make loads of money as a fortune teller?

'Oi, Pablo!' whispered Donald again.

'What?'

'You OK?'

'Mmm, just thinking.'

'Hey, how 'bout you find out what I'm going to get for my birthday!'

I groaned. 'Donald! There's got to be more interesting things I can predict than *that*.'

'Oh, go on. Please?'

I came out of the cubicle. 'Look, I need to experiment a bit…'

Donald gave me a look that said *'what? Not even for your best mate?'* So eventually I said, 'Oh all right. I'll try. But no guarantees, OK?'

Donald gave me a gentle punch on the arm. 'That's the stuff. It's on Sunday, don't forget.'

* * *

So much for my homework that night; it did not get done. Once I got started on finding out stuff about the next few days, there was no holding me back. I couldn't stop drawing whatever came into my head.

'So what am I getting?' asked Donald, chasing after me at lunchtime the next day.

'A new Arsenal kit…'

'Yesss!'

'…And some games. Oh, by the way, your aunty's going to give you a smart outfit.'

'Oh no, not another navy blazer!' groaned Donald. 'Hey, I wish you could come paintballing on Saturday. I swear, *nobody's* as strict as your 'rents about that stuff!'

'Well, you never know…' I said, smiling.

'What? Don't tell me they're gonna *let* you?!'

'Heck, no. But…I discovered that Aunt Dot's going to

have a surprise for them tomorrow night; some last-minute tickets to this *mega* art preview on Saturday. They've been wanting to go, see, and Dot's been trying to wangle some tickets. So I decided to see if I could find out whether she succeeds, and sure enough, I drew her producing the tickets. It's an all day thing, and of course they'll plan to bring me along.'

'Er…and that's *good?*'

'No, stupid, but here's what I'm thinking: tomorrow I start coughing a bit. Then by Friday I'm like, "Mum, I'm not feeling too well, croak croak," but I *soldier on* bravely into school. So, of course by Saturday—'

'OK, I get the picture, you throw a sickie. Then what? You're hardly going to get them to let you go paintballing, for heaven's sake!'

I put my arm around him. 'Ah, but that's where your excellent brother comes into it…'

*   *   *

Yes, I was really beginning to warm to this whole predicting lark. And my plan? It worked like a *dream*. Knowing about those tickets in advance really helped; there's no way I'd have fooled anyone if I tried to pull a sickie right after Aunt Dot produced them. No way! And Mum and Dad were both dead keen to go to this thing, so when I told them Cornelius wouldn't mind hanging out with me for a few hours, they jumped at the chance. Except of course he didn't, did he? No, he whizzed me over to the paintballing party. Donald and I didn't tell him the bit about my folks thinking I was home in bed, though. Oh no, too dodgy. I mean, I know he was in on the whole 'Chess Club' con-trick, but this would probably have been taking it a bit too far. Donald just asked him nicely if he could pick me up and drop me home, and since he'd taken the day off work to help, and it was on the way, he was cool with it.

As a little present for him, I did some homework and found out there was this girl he'd fancied for ages – but who *everyone* fancied – and she was going to dump her boyfriend on Thursday week. And she was going to the Audio Gold disco bar with her mates the next night…Of course, he gave me that sideways look of his like I was completely barking, but I could practically read the 'to do' list he was mentally composing on the spot…

Oh yes, I was feeling *go-o-o-d!* I was even, dare I say it, feeling a little bit superhero-ish. Don't forget, I *never* got to go to birthday parties; footie, swimming, go-karting… You name it, I've missed out on it. And then had to hear all about it on Monday at school. I remember once telling my parents about paintballing. 'You mean, people actually shoot little packages of paint at each other?' said Dad, horrified. 'Whatever for?'

'For *fun*, Dad.'

Dad made that bad-taste-in-the-mouth face. 'What a lamentable misuse of a glorious medium!'

'Ah,' Mum chirped up hopefully. 'Perhaps they *exhibit* their costumes afterwards, is that it?'

'No, Mum. It's *just for fun*.'

This sent them into such confusion, with much blinking and shaking of heads, I thought they might short-circuit there for a moment. If there wasn't some sort of worthy end-product, they just didn't get it.

Paintballing was just the *best*; I'll never forget that day as long as I live. If you've done it, you'll have some idea what I'm talking about. You're out there in this field, and it's like being in a real live battle, only no one gets killed or even hurt, and there's all these obstacles…it is just so cool. I didn't feel guilty at all; I'd won a small battle of my own – hey, I *deserved* to have a good time for once!

But I will always remember that day for another reason, too. Because that was the high point; the one precious moment when it was all going swimmingly. Through a combo of wit, clairvoyance and, er, deviousness, I had triumphed; I was a *winner*, and it was going to be onwards and upwards from here. What a feeling! Completely alien to me, I can tell you; I had to pinch myself to check I wasn't dreaming. It would never have occurred to me at that point, that the dream could turn into a nightmare…

Eight

'Look, I promise you, we've nothing to lose!' insisted Donald, his hand pressing into my back, urging me forward.

I looked at my watch. 'This had better be quick; Mum and Dad'll kill me if they find out I'm gone. We're going off to this gallery at, like, one or something.'

'Then stop dawdling!'

Saturday, one week later: Donald had something he wanted to try out, and here was I, going along with it. I'd had a bit of fun during the week predicting who was going to be number one that week and stuff, so I suppose there was only one thing this was all going to lead to…

It hadn't been too hard to sneak out. As you know, I get left alone in my room for long stretches of time. Dad was working in his shed, and Mum was having a long conversation with Dot about how depressed she was; I figured that for half an hour they wouldn't notice. But I was nervous about the thing we were about to do. I'd never been in a betting shop, and even though I knew Cornelius worked there, I was anxious. But Donald was so hyped up over his idea, and if I'm absolutely honest I was pretty excited too. Between us we'd managed to put together twelve pounds and seventy-six pence. Donald had put his plan into motion the night before. He'd collected a bunch of pictures of the Arsenal and Chelsea football teams, particularly the players who usually scored goals. He'd even found a picture of the stadium. 'Draw the match,' he'd said. 'Just do whatever comes into your head. Then we bet on your prediction. Easy!'

So I had a go. It was the first time I'd tried to predict something that was not directly connected to my own life, or Donald's, so I had to focus really hard on the pictures of those players, soak myself in them. But even after I'd drawn a goal to each side, along with a few other details like penalties, injuries and so on, I still didn't know if it really meant anything.

'But what if I've read the signs all wrong?' I argued, as we wove through the street full of Saturday shoppers. 'I've not tried anything like this before.'

'OK, so we have £12.76 to lose if you're wrong. But I don't see how you can be! A goal's a goal. How can a ball going into a net mean anything except a ball going into a net? And think how much we might win! I saw in the paper this morning, the odds were 3-1 that there'd be a draw, right? Since you think each team will score one goal, that's a draw, and according to my calculator we'll get…' he fished around in his pocket for a grubby slip of paper as we arrived at the doorway to the betting shop. '…Thirty-eight pounds and twenty-eight pee!' He pushed the door open. 'After you, sir!'

I stepped nervously forward.

It was like those cartoon western scenes when the character goes into the saloon and the whole place stops and stares. I turned around, but Donald had my shirt twisted in his grip and was pulling me inside.

There was a cloud of smoke hanging just about level with my head. I coughed. The room was empty of furniture, except for two tellies and a ledge along two of the walls, where assorted crumpled men stood with coats and newspapers and bits of paper. Along the back wall were three windows, like in banks, and more crumpled men were queuing there. I could just make out Cornelius behind one of them. Donald waved at him eagerly, and Cornelius saw us, but didn't smile. Some of the men sniggered, most of them went back to their newspapers or bits of paper or watching the telly. Donald led me across the room to join the queue at Cornelius's window, but before we even got there, Cornelius appeared at Donald's side and grabbed him by the collar.

'What the heck do you think you're doing here?' he hissed.

'We wanted to place a bet,' said Donald, his high-pitched voice setting off a ripple of grown-up laughter.

'You stupid squirt, you know the rules!'

'Yeah, but I just thought—'

'You thought *wrong!*' growled Cornelius. 'Now get out this minute or I'll tell Dad!'

I wanted to die. And I wanted to throttle Donald for doing this to me. One of the men who stood nearby was grinning on one side of his face, his blue eyes piercing mine. My cheeks flushed and I stared at the filthy floor. Funny how sometimes thoughts pop into your head that don't belong to the situation you're in; like right now all I could think was how this man didn't fit his surroundings. He was all spick and span with shoes like shiny conkers and coat the colour of sand dunes, all smooth and perfect and sitting in the middle of this rubbish tip.

Cornelius got us both by the scruff of our necks and steered us to the door. Donald twisted and tried to whisper in his ear, 'But we *know* the result. You could do it for us!'

'Get *out!*' repeated Cornelius, as he shoved us into the street. 'Sorry Pablo,' he added in a softer tone. 'But Donald knows he's not allowed…you have to be over eighteen.'

Donald grew bolder now we were away from all the staring men. 'You wait and see. Arsenal v. Chelsea. It's a draw, 1-1. Pablo knows.'

But Cornelius already had his back to us and was heading inside. I could see the fury in Donald's face as he whirled around and pushed the flapping door. 'OK slaphead,' he snapped. 'Etienne Francois goes off, you'll see. Second half, crunched knee. Try betting on *that!* Ha ha. *Yeah!'*

'Donald!' I hissed as I pulled him back out.

Donald's cheeks bloomed hotly. *'Well!'* he said, in that trying-to-justify-your-wrongness way. As if WELL just made everything WELL again, like a computer instruction.

'You don't *know…'* I began, then I saw the time. 'Oh man, I've got to go.' I stormed off down the street.

'Pablo!' called Donald. 'I'm sorry. I didn't mean to—'

I marched on ahead.

'Sorry,' he repeated as he caught up with me.

'I'm so embarrassed!' I snapped.

'OK, so he got me narked. It's just he, he's always so—'

''S'no excuse to show off like that.'

'Aw, come on Pabs, you've got to admit it was a pretty wicked idea!' said Donald, skipping sideways. He managed to skip right into a baker delivering bread to a restaurant, knocking several rolls to the ground.

'Oi! Why don't you watch where you're going?' yelled the baker.

'Sorry,' said Donald meekly, trying to replace the rolls on the crate.

'Get outta here!' snapped the baker, waving him off. I went to grab a couple of rolls, just to clear them up, when a gleaming pair of leather shoes appeared before me. Conker-brown slip-ons with tassels; it was the man from the betting shop.

'Can't make some bread, so thought you'd *nick* some eh? Heh, heh!' His voice was all spit and tobacco.

We stood up. 'It was an accident,' said Donald. We wanted to move on, but the man was blocking our way.

'You're a sharp one, aintcha, eh? Ha ha! I like that. Frustrating, isn't it, being a minor, when all you want to do is make a few quid.' He made a money-caressing gesture with his fingers. 'But you know, I might be able to help you out, lads. With the bet, like. You give me the dosh, I place your bet, you get the winnin's, Bob's yer uncle!'

'I've got to go,' was all I could say.

'Thanks, sir,' said Donald, just as anxious to get away, 'but we've changed our minds, haven't we Pablo?' He stepped aside, but his way was blocked again.

'Oh lads, *lads!* Now do I look like the kind of geezer's gonna just take your money and scarper? Tuh! How much you got? A tenner is it?'

'Twelve pounds and seventy-six pence,' said Donald. 'Look, I—'

'Ha ha ha!' wheezed the man. 'D'you know 'ow much this coat cost me? Go on, 'ave a guess!'

'Look it's very kind of you to offer,' I blurted out. 'But we really have changed our minds, and we've got to go!' And I grabbed Donald by the arm, slipped round the side of the cigar-scented beige coat, and ran. It wasn't until I got home that I noticed something was missing. The folded sheets of paper which had been in my jacket pocket and now weren't. The sheets of paper that showed one goal to Arsenal, one goal to Chelsea, three penalties, one substitute player. Gone.

Nine

I reckon this was the first time Donald ever really made me mad. I mean, yeah, I get a bit narked with him sometimes, 'cause you just do, don't you? And sometimes we'll have a pretend fight. There's this insult game we play; 'Take That Back!' You know that one? Your friend says, 'You smell of squirrel vomit,' or something. And you yell, 'Take that back!' and he has to try and say it backwards:

Timov lerriuqs fo llems uoy.

Try it. You have to really make the sound backward, as if sucking it in with a Hoover (which, incidentally, is also a useful trick for pretending you can speak Russian, if you're good enough). Well, this time I really wanted him to take it back. Suck in that speech bubble, un-say it, grab those words as they hung in that betting shop smoke-cloud, and shove them in his pocket, safe, before anyone had time to make sense of them.

I lay flat on the bed, staring at the ceiling and the Daffy Duck-shaped patch where I brought down the mobile eight years ago. At least *I* can see Daffy Duck in it, but that's just me: not everyone would. And if you didn't know who Daffy Duck was in the first place, you definitely wouldn't. Perhaps it was the same with what Donald blurted out in the betting shop, I tried to tell myself: since nobody there actually *knew* I could predict things, maybe there wasn't anything to worry about after all. Those guys probably wouldn't have made any sense out of it. And who's going to take any serious notice, I figured, when they probably think we're just a pair of silly boys? No one! Then I thought about the drawings, and a lump formed in my gut. That was the scary part; someone probably did know now, and I *so* did not want that. That one person would no doubt find this very, very interesting indeed. Not so very likely to keep it to themselves. More likely go to the newspapers. Oh no, I thought; I don't want to be famous! I imagined the headlines: **BOY TELLS FUTURE!** and me splashed all over the front page. What a terrifying thought. I don't think famous people have a good time of it at all, 'cause they can't just do whatever they want. Pick your nose or fart and next day the whole world knows about it. And something like this, well, who knew where it would all end? I might get roped in by the secret service or something awful like that. I could just imagine the story:

12-YEAR-OLD SEER EMPLOYED
BY THE GOVERNMENT

To interview young Pablo Hobbs, the world-famous fortune-teller, we visited him in a top secret location somewhere in darkest Essex. 'I miss school,' says Pablo, wistfully tugging on his silken, diamond-encrusted robes. 'I miss playing footie with my mates. I'm well looked-after, and nobody tells me off when I eat the chocolate first then the biscuit part of the Twix and leave the gooey caramelly bit till last and get really messy. But with the future of the planet in my hands, I feel that it's all a bit too much for a twelve-year-old to have to cope with. It's too much responsibility, plus I don't get to ride my bike in the park.' As tears rolled down his face...

'Pablo?'

'Uh, yeah Mum? I answered, blinking myself back to reality but making my best attempt at a sort of been-here-all-the-time type voice.

'We're leaving soon, do you want a sandwich?'

I looked at my watch: 12.45. Mum was being all organized and punctual for once. Phew! Lucky I got back when I did; five minutes later and all hell would have let loose. Then I thought about the match; it would have started by now. My head tingled. Let Arsenal win, I thought. Let Chelsea win. Let it be three-nil, or two-nil, let Francois last the whole match, let me be wrong, wrong wrong. Then everything'll be normal and hunky-dory and predictable – no! Unpredictable.

* * *

The suspense was unbearable, as I trailed around the gallery with Mum and Dad. The one good thing about the way I felt, was that when we came to the silliest thing in the exhibition – and it really was very silly, let me tell you – I didn't laugh, and normally it would have been very, very difficult not to.

'Aha!' said Dad. 'And in this room we have "Juggernaut". We followed a small group through the doorway, but as I looked on the walls I could see nothing at all. Then as we neared the centre of the room, I saw what everyone was looking at. It was a man dressed as a giant rabbit – I kid you not – and he was sitting in a room-set, doing everyday things like making a cup of tea, or doing the washing-up. Straight up! And not a juggernaut in sight.

'Hmm,' said Dad, as he gazed thoughtfully at the scene. Because even though it practically yelled SILLY! at you, no, this was not theatre, it wasn't panto, and it wasn't meant to be funny, so if you burst out laughing you were in dead trouble. Fortunately I knew this, 'cause Dad had taught me to recognise this sort of thing as an art installation. It's Art, so you're meant to stand and stare and make sure you've got a thoughtful expression on your face. A sort of half-smile is permitted; I could see a few people doing exactly this. It tells everyone around you that even though the joke is extremely sophisticated and difficult to understand, you get it. Then you can nod sagely and go back out into the world knowing that– yes! – it's official: you really are better than all the other dull, ordinary people, and doesn't that just make you radiate specialness!

Tense though I was, the temptation to sidle up to the giant rabbit and go, 'What's up, Doc?' was great. It would have been just brilliant to pop the balloon of pretension in that room. As it turned out, someone else did the job for me. An elderly lady in a wheelchair raised a gnarled hand and pointed at Rabbit-Man. 'You ought to be ashamed of yourself!' she croaked. The man ignored her, and continued ironing a shirt. 'You arrogant man!' the woman continued, getting louder. The man pushing the chair, probably her son, went bright red and started to wheel her away.

'I can see through you, don't think I can't!' shrieked the lady, craning her neck as she was forced to leave. Rabbit-man didn't even glance up. 'He's a fraud!' the old gal announced loudly, ignoring the shushes from her son. 'It's all a con-trick…and it's nothing whatever to do with juggernauts!'

It cheered me up, it did. Ha, never expected that. I actually forgot about the footie match for a little while. Some of the people shuffled and murmured uncomfortably, others chuckled softly and said things like, 'Poor old dear,' and 'Obviously not quite right,' indicating their heads with circular finger movements.

We were still discussing it when we got home. 'I still don't get why it's called "Juggernaut",' I said.

'Sometimes you have to think laterally,' explained Dad, 'something that poor old lady obviously never learnt to do. Quite apart from being off her trolley.'

'Yes, but why…?'

'If art must be explained verbally, Pablo, then it has failed. I have faith in your intelligence—'

'Oh!' I cried and dived for the radio, suddenly remembering the match. It would be over by now, and – excellent timing – I'd just managed to catch the 5 o'clock news bulletin. 'Sorry, Dad.'

'As I was saying,' Dad continued, 'I believe you're bright enough to work it out for yourself.'

I attempted to listen to both him and the radio at the same time. 'Suppose I'm not, though? Does that mean

I'm not worthy of it? Why does it have to be a puzzle, why can't it be for everyone?'

'*And now, with a round-up of the day's soccer results, here's Dennis Keeper,*' went the radio.

'Pablo...'

'Ssh!' I hissed, before I knew what I was doing. 'Sorry, I just want to know what happened...'

Dad blinked at me, then shook his head and picked up the newspaper.

'*...and at Stamford Bridge, a strong start for Arsenal thanks to Lorenzo Avlini's early goal, which left the score at one-nil...*'

One-nil!

'*...for most of the match, with van Hoegaarden only scoring the equaliser for Chelsea in the eightieth minute...*'

Oh, man!

'*...Etienne Francois, who was injured in the second half of the match, is nursing a torn ligament in his right knee, and it's unclear as yet whether he'll be fit to play in Wednesday's away match against Barnsley.*'

Well, that's it then, I thought. My secret was out. All of a sudden, being 'gifted' didn't feel like fun any more; it felt like a ball and chain. Here I was, an apparently normal person, going about doing normal things, except there was one really not-normal thing about me – something I could get headhunted for. Suddenly the man in the rabbit suit made perfect sense, and I thought, he's talking about me!

Good grief, I thought: I actually get it. So why am I not radiating specialness? And why do I still not get the "Juggernaut" part?

Ten

I fell asleep at eight o'clock or something ridiculous; I guess all that tension just burns you up after a while. But when I woke up, it was only two-thirty, and let me tell you I was WIDE awake. There were so many thoughts to be thunk, so much unfinished business. I crept downstairs and had a glass of milk and two cookies. Then I headed back towards the stairs. Do some drawing, I thought. If I'm that worried about what will happen next, well, why not just draw the future, see what happens? But something was holding me back; fear, I guess. I went back and ate three more cookies.

Now I wished I'd spoken to Donald; when he'd phoned about the match results I'd pretended to be busy. I sat on the couch and pressed my nose against the windowpane, watching my breath give a spooky, graveyard effect to the moonlit garden. Well, call it a garden, more a like rubbish tip. There's all the scrap metal that Dad's collected over the years but has yet to do anything with. There's old paint pots and brushes that Mum will one day get around to taking to the dump. There's a broken bike, and there's a lot of weeds.

And beyond all that is Dad's shed.

I'm not allowed in Dad's shed; no one is. He locks it up, but as he just hangs the key on a hook by the back door, I could easily get in if I wanted to. Suddenly I wanted to; it might take my mind off things for a bit. And yes, I was curious; just what *did* he do in there? He seemed to be doing a lot less painting these days; the black lines were apparently leading nowhere. But he spent an awful lot of time holed up in that shed.

Creeping across the dewy, overgrown grass, I thought blimey! Here I am, sneaking out for the second time in twenty-four hours. What's that all about, then? As I got nearer, I was surprised at how excited I was, and then I realised why: I just didn't *know* him. For all his showy talk, what did he ever really communicate? Couldn't he once, just once, do dad-stuff, like on the Soppy Film Channel? You know, wear a plaid shirt with the sleeves rolled up, ruffle my hair, punch me on the shoulder and call me 'kid', arm-wrestle me? I'd so LOVE that. Not to mention a bit of footie once in a while. As I put the key in the padlock, I had slushy songlines in my head, all that 'let me unlock the key to your heart' stuff, and if this was a cheesy music video, I expect the door would now swing open to reveal, to reveal...

What? Some sculptures, yes. But they were covered in dust. Tools on the bench, a soldering iron. Some doodles. Piles of yellowing newspapers, a radio. Books. What was he working on *now?* A crossword, apparently. I searched on the bench, under it, all over, but couldn't find any great work in progress. I flipped through the doodle-pad: blank page after blank page. I sat in the ripped old swivel chair and stared at the newspaper with the half-finished crossword and the filthy coffee mug beside it. The place smelled mouldy. *This* is what my dad does.

Well, he might not be the chummy, arm-wrestling type of dad, might be a bit aloof and all that, but right away I knew one thing for sure: he wasn't being idle. Idleness is a happy tra-la-la kind of thing, and there's no way my dad was happy. Besides, I knew he had a strict routine: idle people don't do that. No, all that dreary nothingness was down to the dreary nothingness in my dad's head: he'd run out of ideas.

Somehow this realization made my face go all hot. One person you absolutely don't ever want to feel sorry for is your dad. No! Just the thought of it is positively skin-crawly, like seeing your granny naked or something. The whole lumpy sadness of it weighed me down, and now I wished I'd never gone into that shed.

And yet I found I couldn't leave; I was transfixed by that blank doodle-pad. It winked at me; such a perfectly clear, shiny new surface like a glassy pool, ready to be dived into. I tried to tear myself away, but the urge was too great and I had experienced enough to know that this was because a prediction was coming, and there was nothing I could do to hold it back. In a moment I was off the diving board and hurtling towards the water. Only if I was a cartoon might I have hung there in mid-air, changed my mind and swooped back up onto the board. But this is the real world, and just as you can't unsay things you've already said, so there comes a point when you know the ball will hit that window, this person will do a bellyflop.

It was as if something else was controlling my hand, furiously scribbling away and I'm thinking crikey! I'm possessed by some demon! It was that bonkers. There was a whole wacky bunch of nonsense at first. It reminded me of the stuff you hear about Ouija boards. I've never done it, but I thought about Donald's neighbour's cousin whose cat died after a ghost told her it would happen. It felt spooky, it made my neck clammy.

It kept going and now a whole page was filled with a mish-mash of letters, symbols and shapes. And gradually the drawing became less frantic and clearer images came through. This is what I drew:

Then I filled another whole page, but it all began to make less and less sense to me; it didn't seem to be telling a story any more. It was turning back into mish-mash:

Eleven

'I'm going to be kidnapped.'

'You're what?'

'I'm going to be kidnapped,' I repeated. 'I know it, I've seen the future and it's all here in my backpack. Someone's out to get me.'

'Tsss!' went Donald. 'Don't talk rot. You're paranoid, man! I knew we never should've watched that *X-Files* thing.' He reached for my backpack. 'Here, lemme see.'

I clamped it to my chest. 'Uh-uh, not here.' Other kids were beginning to thunder into the locker room. 'Tomorrow at yours, Chess Club.'

'Hey, if you're right, you might've been kidnapped by then!' He'll make a good lawyer one day, will Donald. I gave him the drawings and he snuck them into the loo.

By the time he came out, the bell had gone for a second time and everyone else had bolted. I knew we'd get detention, but I didn't care.

Donald didn't seem bothered, either. He waved the first page at me. 'OK, you know what this stuff looks like to me? It's you putting your worries into pictures. This isn't a prediction, you're just expressing yourself, that's all.'

'But—'

'Let me finish. The second page proves it, because it couldn't possibly be a prediction. It doesn't make any sense! All those ghosts and funny faces…they're doodles! There's no story there at all.'

I frowned angrily at him. 'So how do you explain them then? I tell you Donald, something was inside me when I was drawing those. I wasn't just sitting there, you know, blah-de-blah, talking on the telephone. I practically passed out afterwards!'

'You're not making any sense to me.'

'It's a feeling. I can't explain…'

'Yes, it's called PA-RA-NOI-A,' he interrupted. Then he softened. 'Look, about the betting shop, I don't see how anyone would seriously —'

'What about that man that came up to us in the street, then?'

'Aah, that old codger? You're scared of him? He was just trying to help, that's all.'

'Oh yeah?' I gave him a piercing look. 'So why'd he pinch my drawings?'

Donald squinted. 'He what?'

'I think he stole my drawings of the match. When I got home they were gone.'

Donald paused, then shrugged. 'Hey, they probably just fell out of your pocket when you were dashing home.'

I held my head and groaned. 'OK, OK but look: what if they didn't?'

After that Donald stuck to me like glue. He made sure I was never on my own outside school, so either he or Cornelius was with me at all times. I don't think he filled Cornelius in exactly, just told him I had a bad reaction to *The X-Files*. Which is what he truly thought deep down, I reckon. Plus he probably didn't believe anything as front page as a kidnapping could really happen to his best mate. Me, on the other hand, I could imagine it only too well. That's the trouble with having a vivid imagination; sometimes it sits there in your belly like a nasty little purple gremlin with yellow teeth going, 'I need more worries! Feed me!' And even though you know it's just your imagination, that doesn't stop His Purpleness from kicking around in there, tying your guts in knots. And the more worries you feed him, the hungrier he gets. At the House Of Tellies, he actually went to sleep for a while, the little horror. We watched TOONS, lots of 'em, and I escaped into the Arizona desert! The City of Townsville! Under-the Sinksville, N.J! It was B.L.I.S.S. But the minute the telly screen was dark, he was up and at 'em, and tantrumming again like a two-year-old.

* * *

71

I didn't draw any cartoons. I didn't draw anything, I was so worried, 'cause it seemed I had no control any more over what came out on the page. I might start out drawing Richie Roach, and along would come some Bogey Man without even knocking on the door; just leap right into the picture and start biting heads off and who knows what else. Little old Yellow-Tooth Gremlin would see to that. And I still couldn't get to grips with the feeling I'd had in Dad's shed, that feeling of something taking over. I couldn't work out whether it was pain or pleasure I had felt. One thing I was sure of: it freaked me out.

Wednesday: Nothing out of the ordinary (still not drawing).

Thursday: ditto.

Friday: ditto again. But old Purple-Face seemed to be shrinking ever so slightly. I began to see things in a different light; if not quite Soppy-movie-channel-sun-kissed-gold, then at least not *X-Files* rain-soaked-black either. Somewhere in between. Accelerating cars didn't have me jumping five feet in the air any more. And part of me started to believe Donald's version of things; perhaps I really was paranoid.

Who knows where all that weird stuff came from? Perhaps Dad's shed was haunted.

Hey, there's a thought. I should tell him that: 'Dad, you've gotta go down there at night, meet the shed ghost, he's got loads of ideas! No more sitting there racking your brains.' And he'd do it, and the ghost would get inside his skin and all of a sudden he'd be hammering and soldering and sparking up a storm, and before long he'd have this big exhibition and sell loads of stuff, and make a million pounds! And there I'd be, glowing with pride, saying, 'That's my Dad!'

Oh, back to reality. Friday night was Detention Night. Yeah, last day of term and they still had to get in that bit of punishment for loitering in the locker room on Monday. Donald and I had to write essays about 'What Would Happen To Society If Everyone Behaved The Way We Did'. I wasted a lot of time, because I couldn't resist writing a whole discussion about how actually, breaking the rules is sometimes daring, brave and admirable, and by the way, look where it got Pablo Picasso. He was always breaking the rules, didn't do him any harm, did it? Or society, for that matter. Then I showed it to Donald and he just shook his head slowly. So I tore it up and started again with a load of old tosh about how the whole world would collapse in a heap if people didn't obey the rules. It meant Donald finished way before me, but he and Cornelius hung around. Then they were making too much noise in the hallway, so Miss Tite went and told them to go and wait in the school office.

A little while later, she began sighing heavily as she put her marking away noisily, making sure I knew *she* was done with *her* work, thank you very much. 'Pablo, it's five thirty. I need you to finish up now, please.'

73

'Oh, I'm almost done, honest!' I can't deny it, I was getting a lot of fun out of watching her get more and more narked, 'specially since it looked like she had a hot date. She was wearing her swanky boots, and kept taking out her mirror to fix her lipstick and do her hair so the front bit fell forward just so. I almost forgot about Donald and Cornelius, it was so much fun. Then, when I finally stood up to bring my work over, she didn't notice at first and seemed deeply engrossed in something. I just caught a glimpse of a mobile phone before she spotted me coming over and tried to shove it in her bag but missed. It clattered to the floor and I rushed to pick it up for her.

'No! Um…that's all right, I can—' she stuttered, face turning crimson.

I just caught a few words on the phone's little glowing screen: CANT W8 2 C U SEXYBUM before she snatched it, gathered everything up and bolted for the door.

'Miss, don't forget this!' I called after her, waving my essay.

She turned, hair now mostly in front of her face, which made her look slightly insane. 'Oh. Thank you.'

'Miss,' I said, just as she was turning again.

She huffed. 'What?'

'The no-phones-in-class rule. Does that go for teachers as well?'

'I…it's. I've got a train to catch, you've delayed me quite enough!' And she bolted, almost falling over her swanky boots in the process.

I was still chuckling to myself on the way to the locker room. Lucky for her she didn't come this way, I thought, as I headed into the west wing, where the newly-mopped floor was particularly slippery.

'Sorry,' I said to the cleaner as I passed him.

He glanced back at my footprints on the wet floor, a weary-looking old guy I hadn't seen before. 'No matter, mate,' he replied.

I carried on my way, then all of a sudden an awful familiar sickening feeling hit the pit of my belly.

My Purple Gremlin. Something about his hands had struck me: LOVE and HATE tattooed on the fingers, and now I realised what I was scared of; those hands, this corridor; they were in my drawings of the kidnap.

I quickened my pace, ears pricking up as I heard the clunk of the cleaner picking up his bucket – the bucket! There had been a bucket in the drawings! I could feel him following me – oh, stay calm! – as I worked out how far I needed to go. Ahead were some steps; up those, out the door, across the terrace, down some more steps and across the car park. I decided to make a dash for it, and took the steps two by two. *Clunk*! I heard the bucket hit the floor, and now quickening footsteps – *quick for an old man* – and just as I got to the double doors he was upon me and a big hanky with a pungent jelly-bean smell was clamped to my face.

Oh, where was Miss Tite now that I needed her? I struggled and kicked and thrashed, but my heart sank at the sight of the red tail-lights of her car as it left the car park. Suddenly I was hot and weak and everything was going fuzzy. The last thing I remember is my arms and legs wilting like noodles and that, as they say, was that.

Twelve

When I came to, I was a tight parcel rattling around in a large box. Hands behind my back, face silenced. My head ached and my eyes itched, which was driving me crazy. The box was apparently moving, and eventually I realised it was the back of a van. Just as I had predicted. Then it wasn't moving any more, there was a clunk, clunk, and footsteps. The door opened.

'Mah MAN. How's it goin', bro?' The voice was oil-slick deep. A big face with dark wrap-around glasses loomed toward me, teeth glinting with gold, and there was a huge hand with gold bracelet and gold rings. 'Put it there, man. Oops, ah forgot! You can't, can you?'

'Roight!' said another, higher voice. 'Better get 'im in, like. Come on!' This one took a gleaming knife and cut the rope at my ankles; LOVE and HATE joined forces to release my legs. Those same hands: the cleaner, only not an old man any more – that had obviously been a disguise.

'Enjoy the ride, didja?'

I scowled at him.

We were in a dingy garage. I was led up a couple of steps, through a door and across a hallway all green marble and gilt. A familiar gravelly voice from inside a room called out, 'The nipper's here, eh?' And I knew instantly it was the man from the betting shop. 'Fanbleedin'tastic!' he said as he appeared in the doorway, leaning on the door-frame casual as you like, grinning from ear to ear. 'You can undo him now, fellas.'

They did so, but kept a firm grip on my arms.

'I don't believe we've introduced ourselves properly,' said the man as he stepped closer and offered me his hand. 'L.J Sylva.'

I went to bite his hand, but he pulled it away quickly. The other two tightened their grip.

'Oh, now now, don't let's get off on the wrong foot, eh? Here, come an' sit down, there's a lad.' He ushered me and two of my closest friends into the room, and offered me a seat in front of a large desk. The big guy sat next to me.

'Fink yer need this,' said L.J, handing me a tissue. He gave me a moment to wipe my itchy, wet eyes. 'That's the chloroform,' he explained. 'You'll be back to normal in no time. We'll get you some Sprite or something. Bronzo? Get the lad a Sprite.'

'Boss,' said Bronzo, the one with the love/hate relationship with his hands. I watched him go to a mini fridge in the corner. He was still as bald as he'd been in his disguise, only now his head had sprouted bits of metal all over the place. Spikes and studs, rings like belt buckles, Frankenstein bolts. He must have spent the whole journey putting them back in. Must have worn a latex mask as well, or very expert make-up.

'So,' oozed L.J, 'you know my name, how about you tell us yours?'

'No Sprite, boss, only Tango,' said Bronzo.

L.J waved his hand. 'Yur, Tango, whatever. Now, lad. Looks like we're going to get acquainted, so if yer don't mind—'

'Oh, it's not Tango, it's Fanta.'

'I don't care if it's Fan-bleedin'Dango, just give the lad a drink!' barked L.J.

A stifled laugh came from Gold Teeth next to me. Bronzo hissed at him.

'While we're on the subject of introductions,' L.J continued, 'this 'ere is Bronzo. He may not know his soft drinks, but then soft he ain't. 'Ard as nails, is Bronzo, and vicious as a Rottweiler.'

Bronzo put the Fanta down and pulled the ring. It hissed at me.

'And my esteemed colleague to your right is known as Bling. On account of all the joolery, like.'

'Yo,' said Bling, raising a gold-encrusted hand.

'I was once a medallion man,' said L.J 'But y'know, I'm too old for all that now. 'Preciate the finer things in life, though, I do. You might of noticed. 'Ow about you, Mickey? Like nice things, do you? Smart trainers? Video games? Eh, Mickey?'

I glanced over my shoulder, but then I realised he was talking to me. His strange, lop-sided stare didn't help. I mumbled, 'My name's not Mickey.'

L.J came around the desk towards me. 'Whassat? Did you say something, Mickey?'

'I said my name's not Mickey.' I could feel the tears welling up again in my eyes.

'Aah! Now we're getting somewhere! What *is* your name then?'

'It's Pablo.'

Pablo! D'you hear that, Bling? Pablo! That's very, ah, appropriate, innit? Quite the artist, aren't you, Pablo?' He pulled a piece of paper from the desk and dangled it in front of me. 'This your work?'

I hesitated. 'No,' I said.

L.J tutted and gave a sharp intake of breath. 'That's a pity,' he said, as he turned and walked around the desk. 'Perhaps you'll enlighten us as to *who* the *hartist* is, in that case?'

At this moment, Bronzo and Bling did their tough guy poses, eyes burning, casting heavy shadows and causing me to go *gulp!* just like Jerry does whenever Tom gets hold of him. Bronzo pulled a chain attached to his belt and began fiddling with the Swiss Army knife at the end of it.

'All right, it's me!' I said at last. 'But it doesn't mean anything, now let me go!'

'That's more like it!' beamed L.J. He snapped open a silver cigar case and leaned forward. 'Cigar?'

I must have given him such a filthy look.

'Oooh, no mister!' he teased, lighting one for himself. My drawing: the man with the cigar. It was all in there; Bronzo, Bling, the lot. L.J's cheeks disappeared into Y-shaped creases as he puffed. 'Been smoking since I were nine, me. Nice to do business over a stogie, I always think. Relaxing. Gets the grey cells circulating. And that's what we're here for, Pablo: business. See, we could make a nice little team, you and me. You and your mate; 'scuse me, but you ain't got a clue about gambling!' He gave a phlegmy chuckle. 'I mean, fair play, you got the nouse to 'ave a go – I respect that, I do. You worked out what this could do for yer'. He dangled the drawings again, wafting the blue clouds of teabag'n'tarmac-smelling smoke. 'But footie – ha!' He shook his head. 'Naahhh! Waste a time. 'Orses is where it's at. The gee-gees. Any good at maffs, Pablo?'

I said nothing, just stared at the smoke rising from his cigar.

He pulled a slim calculator from his pocket. 'Nah, me neither. And why bother when yer got these, I say. Why bother with school even, when yer could be makin' money? Woss twelve times twenty-five, eh? Wanna guess? No?' He punched some buttons on his calculator.

'Right. Says 'ere, if you and your mate had put your twelve nicker on an 'orse at twenty-five to one, and that 'orse won the race; well you'd a walked away with 300 nicker! How many smart trainers and video games is that, then?'

I gazed at the curls of smoke. With his wicked grin, and smoke trailing around him, he was like a cartoon devil. It reminded me of the Richie Roach episode, in which:

    The Devil is a posh wasp lawyer called B.L. Zebub
    III, who offers Richie escape to a wonderful new
    life, with everything his heart desires!!!

Yeah right, lots of money, very nice; I did not answer.

'Ah, but of course there's the little matter of your age, isn't there, Pablo?' L.J went on. That's where I come in, see? Offerin' you a sort of partnership. Play yer cards right, you could do quite handsome out of this, Pablo. Couldn't he, boys?' Bronzo and Bling, at ease now, both nodded slowly.

'Roight,' said Bronzo.

'Solid,' agreed Bling.

    So Richie, not realising that B.L Zebub III is
    the Devil, reads and signs the legal contract
    offered to him. Right away, his wish comes true
    and he's atop the stinkiest rubbish tip in the

whole of New Jersey, along with his beloved Rosie and an endless supply of XX-tra Hot Salsa. Feelin' hot hot hot!

Then one day, Rosie says, 'Everything's so wonderful. How come?' and Richie shows her the contract. Shock, horror! Rosie says, 'You made a pact with the Devil!' She produces a mega-mega-super-powerful magnifying glass to read the microscopic fine print, which says that Richie agrees to an eternity of damnation in the hell that is the squeakiest cleanest kitchen, constantly under attack from the killer bleach bottle.

'What if I don't want to?' I heard myself say, not daring to look at L.J's face.

'Ah, now that could make things…complicated,' said L.J gravely, pausing for effect so I could imagine just what sort of complicated he meant. 'But before we decide anything,' he added cheerily, 'I bet you're a little tired from your journey. Hungry too, I 'spect. So we're going to take good care of you. I'm famished myself, need a good vindaloo; Bronzo, do the honours will you? Menu's by the phone, the Balti Raj Palace. The usual; make sure mine's got extra hot chilli peppers…'

Hot hot hot!

'...And a korma for the lad.'

Bronzo dialled.

'After that, the boys'll escort you to your quarters,' L.J informed me. 'You'll be nice and comfortable down there. But no funny business—'

'Er, sorry boss, was it onion bhajis you wanted for starters, or samosas?' said Bronzo.

'Samosas,' said L.J. 'Like I say, any funny business—'

'Sorry boss, was that veg or meat samosas?'

'Meat! Meat! Meat!' yelled L.J. 'Gordon Bennett...where was I?'

'Funny business,' prompted Bling helpfully.

L.J puffed thoughtfully on his cigar, then waved it about. 'Never mind. You seem a nice lad. Seems a nice lad, don't he Bling?'

'He's cool.'

'You could learn a thing or two from yer uncle L.J, Pablo. Like, never eat anything that didn't once have a face. Veggies is for pansies.'

'You're not my uncle,' I said into my school sweatshirt.

L.J ignored this, and carried on. 'Now Pablo, I'm a fair man. Whatever you need for making your predictions, just say the word, you got it. Wivin reason. We'll talk after our tea, awright? And tomorrow the fun starts. With the gee-gees. Yeah. You an' me.' He put his arm around me, all pallsy-wallsy. 'We're gonna make a great team.'

Thirteen

Purple Gremlin was at it again, tying my guts in knots and sending me pacing up and down like a caged lion. Do you want to know what my 'quarters' were like? Beige. Airless. No windows, bare lightbulb. Clock with a grinding electronic tick that went *glatch, glatch,* high up on the wall. Big damp patch near the ceiling. Damp-ish mattress in the corner, thin duvet with faded cover. Touchingly, L.J had gone out and bought me brand new pyjamas. The thin scratchy sort, with too-small hole for the head and GOAL! in big letters across the front, and a picture of a player scoring. Ha ha. Sense of humour. On the other side of the heavily-bolted door was Bling parked on a sofa, watching a portable telly. All I could hear was the muffled *psheow, psheow!* of movie gunfire.

I'd predicted the whole thing, and it hadn't done me the slightest bit of good.

And now, here I was, doing what? *Homework.* Of a sort. Because after we'd eaten the Indian food (or at least, *they* had; I just pushed it around my plate) L.J had showed me all the info he had on three of Saturday afternoon's races. 'I know a bloke who trains 'orses,' he'd said. Got you all the bumph.' And he laid it all out in front of me; lots of descriptions of the horses, and the colours the jockeys would be wearing. Everything except pictures; no way could he have got pics of every single horse and jockey. 'Fink you can work with that?' he asked.

I could have said it wasn't enough, that I needed pictures. But where would that get me? Something told me L.J wasn't the type to just say, 'Oh, really? Never mind then, we'll take you home. Sorry to bother you.' No, not L.J: he was going to get a result, one way or another. Then I had another thought: perhaps if I went along with everything, it would help the police to find me. Because if they knew about the betting shop and everything, well they'd be on the lookout for someone making suspiciously high wins, wouldn't they? Just like the time Donald's mum's bag was stolen, and the thief had gone round half a dozen stores, spending money on her credit card before she even knew what had happened. In that case they didn't find the thief 'cause it was too late, he'd moved on. But we weren't going anywhere, as far as I knew. Just co-operate, I decided; then they'll find you.

After an hour or so of studying the information, it was all going blurry in front of my eyes so I stopped. I got into my GOAL! pyjamas and lay down. I couldn't remember the last time I wanted my mum so badly. She might be a sad, depressed zombie of a mum, but she's the only one I've got and I wanted her. I pictured her sitting at the kitchen table blubbing, staring at my picture. Dad too, perhaps, and Aunt Dot. And they'd have got the police out looking for me; perhaps right now they were hot on my trail, and would be hammering on the front door any minute. That's right, they'd have talked to Donald, and he'd have told them all about the betting shop (!), my drawings (!!), my kidnap fears. But I wanted to be rescued. I wanted my poky little room, the crumbly, crumpled couches and toppling piles of stuff, the whole sorry turpentine-stinking swamp that was home. Sounds daft, but I felt dead guilty for all the times I'd wished I lived in a different home. As if by thinking it I'd actually put myself where I was now. I know it's silly, but that's the sort of thing that goes through your head at a time like this. I was like Richie Roach, sitting on top of his glorious pile reading the fine print of his contract and going, 'No! I wanted freedom, but not at this price!' I listened and listened for the police, but they didn't come. What if they couldn't find me? I'd have to escape, or be forced to co-operate with 'Uncle L.J' in his evil plan; my own pact with the devil. But then I told myself: hey, relax, it's the commercial break! Just hang right there in suspended animation until the action resumes in the morning. No one's doing anything terrible to you right now; you can make believe you're at home, and everything's normal. You could even sneak downstairs for a midnight snack if you wanted to…

I thought about that 'Richie Roach and the Devil' episode again. I remembered how, during the commercial break, I'd thought, boy, how's he gonna get out of that one, then? Condemned to an eternity in hell! It's all in the contract – he signed it! There's no way out of that, right? Wrong. What do you think Richie and Rosie did? They OUT-SMARTED the Devil.

Yup. Even B. L Zebub III doesn't think of everything, and first thing Richie and Rosie think is, 'He's a wasp, and we're cockroaches. What are cockroaches good at, that wasps aren't? And that's how they hit on their idea. They got together a great team of Roach Investigators, and scoured every rubbish tip in the entire state of New Jersey. One of them comes back and says, 'I think I've found something very interesting!' He dips his stinkometer into Richie and Rosie's tip (all cockroaches have stinkometers attached to their butts). It measures 80,000 stink-o-bytes, so he goes, 'Yup! Get your Mr Zebub back here, I got something to show him.' B. L Zebub III appears, and the four of them make their way to a dump in Pleasantville.

All three cockroaches dip in their stinkometers. The Pleasantville tip measures a stonking I20,000 stink-o-bytes. It's STINKIER! They've caught the devil out on a technicality; he didn't keep his part of the deal, which was to put Richie atop the stinkiest rubbish tip in New Jersey.

'I believe,' says Richie, 'this renders the agreement null and void. You don't keep your part of the deal, I don't keep mine!' And he tears up the contract right in front of B. L Zebub III.

Brilliant. Whoever said you can't learn anything from telly? All I had to do was out-smart my captors; I did after all have something they didn't have, didn't I?

But without paper and pencils I was like Batman without his bat, Spiderman without his spider…no, hang on… Well, you know what I mean. I might as well have been any old Joe Schmoe, 'cause there was no way they were going to kit me out with the tools of my trade, as L.J would probably call them – not until I was called upon to perform for him. Plus, of course, he'd have realised the stabbing-in-the-eye potential of a nice pointy pencil. No: I was on my own.

If only I had my pictures from before the kidnap! The Shed Drawings, as I'd come to think of them. Maybe they held some clues that would help; I tried my best to remember them exactly. But my head hurt, and I was so fried, I just couldn't focus my thoughts. Oh, it's no use, I thought, slumping onto the mattress. My sleep was filled only with zzz's.

Fourteen

'Well, aren't we dapper!' said L.J, looking me up and down as I entered his study. 'Good threads. Bling picked 'em out special, dincha Bling?'

'Yo.'

And yes, I did look the business. Bling, having his finger on the pulse, had me kitted out in these massive jeans, and probably the hippest T-shirt I'd ever possessed. Obviously calculated to get me in a good mood; Mum made me wear mostly second-hand stuff, or things from discount stores that had probably been the happening thing somewhere at some time (like Albania 1995) and never fitted quite right. So if I'm perfectly honest, it was a pretty clever move on their part. Although their generosity didn't stretch to supplying me with footwear; well I was a prisoner, after all. They'd even confiscated my watch.

'Get the camera, will you Bronzo?'

'Roight.'

'I hope you're feeling pink and perky today, Pablo,' said L.J. 'How about a little flutter, just for fun?'

Bronzo came over with a funny-looking camera and with a blinding flash took my picture.

'What was that for?' I asked.

'All in good time,' said L.J. 'First things first. Done yer homework, have you?' He gave me that twinkly blue-eyed look that said, *you'd better have.*

'Yes,' I mumbled.

'Good. Bronzo? Get the DVD on will you?'

* * *

So here I was, back in the hindquarters of the headquarters with nothing but the *glatch, glatch* of the clock for company. Except I now had a desk, paper and pencils, and all the pages of 'bumph'. Like sitting some rotten exam. Felt fantastic to hold a pencil again though, and I wanted so badly to draw cartoons, but forced myself to concentrate on the race. The DVD we'd watched was other horse races, to give me a feel for the thing. I'd never seen one in my life before; a bit boring, but I could see how you'd be excited about it if you really wanted one particular horse to win.

I looked at the clock; I had two hours.

Boy, these horses had some funny names. Fancy being called Willie Wombat, or even Leggateach Corner (geddit?) How about Frusty Wimple-Bot? I sat, pencil poised, and waited for the story to come. That's how it happens; you concentrate with every atom of your brain on the info you've got, then wait for the rest to download from whatever heavenly website it comes from.

I waited and waited. Nothing. I got up and stretched my legs, padding about in my socks. I asked for a glass of water.

Glatch, glatch.

I sat down again. I stared at the floor. I pulled at my earlobe. I bent down the top of my ear, then let it flip back with a satisfying plop! I did this several times. Nothing.

Glatch, glatch.

Maybe if I start drawing horses, something will happen. I drew horses. La la la. I looked at the clock: 12:23. They'd be coming for me at 1:15; I had less than hour left. I started to prickle all over with panic. Oh no! This was going to make it worse.

I needed the loo. 'Hello?'

'Yo.'

'I need the loo.'

I went to the loo. Came back.

Glatch, glatch.

12:27. Perhaps I'll be rescued before 1:15…then again, perhaps not. I wished some magical little friend would appear – *puff*! – like in cartoons. Oh stop it! Wishing life was like cartoons was not going to help. But you know how it is when someone says to you, 'Don't think of elephants', the elephant is there in your head and it's not going anywhere.

I did a little doodle of Richie Roach, just to get it out of my system. I drew him and the little spider that comes to his aid in the episode 'Salami Spin'. In this episode, Richie's in a fix 'cause he's escaped Under-the-Sinksville, but has run into Sergeant Salami, the sausage guard-dog…

He is amazed to find that the dog has changed character completely, treating Richie like a long-lost friend. Then Sergeant Salami explains that he is now General Salami and is running the whole of Backyardsville. His fab new kennel is five times the size of the old one, and needs decorating. General Salami, who isn't too smart, says to Richie, 'You bugs, you all can do some mighty fine stuff. Spin me some gorgeous webs to decorate the place, make it purdy.'

Richie tries to explain that he can't spin webs, because he's not a spider, but Sergeant Salami just smiles and says, 'I know youse won't let down a good ol' pal now,' and brings him to the

94

Kennel Palace. He presents Richie with a pile of **Woof-Woof** dog biscuits ('valuable currency in these here parts, yes indeedy-doodle!') Richie starts to think, I gotta get away from here. But when he tries to sneak out, he finds he can't; the place is guarded by Soldier Squirrels. He has until tomorrow to spin the webs: what can he do?

Then a little spider appears. 'I'll spin the webs for you, but you've got to pay me.' So Richie gives the spider some of the **Woof-Woof** biscuits, and the spider spins the webs.

Next day, General Salami is delighted, and sticks a badge on Richie. 'Ah offially appoint yew Minister of the Interior,' he says. 'Next thang is rugs. Yessiree Bob, all spun in the finest gossamer and reflectin' the colours of the rainbow. You-all do that for your ol' buddy Slim-Slam, there's a pal.'

And Richie is shut away, and again the little spider comes along and offers to spin the rugs, and again Richie pays him. It is a lot of work, taking the spider all night long, so Richie has to give him the last of the **Woof-Woof** biscuits.

Next day, General Salami is thrilled with the beautiful rugs, but it's still not enough. 'Hmm. Chandeliers, that's what it needs. Big shiny chandeliers, all glintin' in the sunlight. Ain't nothin' like that yarn o' yourn to make em out of, ol' buddy, ol' pal, ol' bud.'

Richie is shut away again. Once more the little spider appears and offers to spin the chandeliers, but Richie has nothing left to pay him with. The spider says, 'Tough luck, sucker! I'm outta here!'

Richie says, 'Hold it right there. I know this story. You think you've got all this power over me, but the spell is broken if I guess your name.'

'Sure,' says the spider, 'but you won't get it!'

'Is it Rumpelstiltskin?' asks Richie.

The spider jumps up and down, cackling. 'No, no, no! You'll never get it! I'm off.'

'No wait! Is it Skimbleshanks? Anansi? Peter Parker?'

'No, no and no!'

'Hang on, is it Charlotte? er...' Richie is sweating buckets at this point. Then, just as the spider is on his way out, cackling his funny little cackle, Richie gets it. 'STOP! Your name is Grickle-Grack.'

The spider is astonished. 'How did you know?'

'Because that is exactly the noise you make when you laugh!'

'Oh drat,' says the spider. 'S'pose I'll have to rescue you now. Come on then.' And Richie climbs onto Grickle-Grack's back and they abseil out the window on the spider's thread, right into the arms of Slomo Flash, who has beaten up the Squirrel Soldiers. He brings Richie back to Under-the-Sinksville, and all the girlies go, 'Oh Slomo, our hero,' etc.

The End.

What did this tell me about my own situation? Precisely zilch, as far as I could tell. At least thinking about Richie calmed me down a bit; what Mum would call 'therapy'. Cleared my head. But I was running out of time. Then, at six minutes past one, just as I had practically abandoned all hope, I found myself drawing again. What came out was this:

I heard the slide of the bolts just as I was finishing the last bit. L.J walked in, followed by Bronzo and Bling. L.J rubbed his hands together. 'Now then, how'd we do?'

I stared at the drawing, trying to make sense of it. L.J snatched it up. 'Wassat then, a camel? Come off it Pablo, there ain't any camels in an 'orse race. What are you, daft or summink?'

I had to admit, it did look suspiciously camel-like.

'And this one 'ere, woss all that about? Why's it got wheels?'

How should I know? I wanted to say. 'Um...'

'Woss this then?' he said pointing to the last one. 'Wings? You 'aving a laugh, are you? Fink this is some kind of joke, do you?' He leaned on the desk and thrust his big, ugly mug right up close, stale tobacco mixed with pine fragrance and yesterday's vindaloo.

Wings...wings. Suddenly I remembered Dr Henderson Spoon, and the drawing I'd done with the slide and the rocks and the cornflakes...the name! The wings had to be something to do with the name. And that tail...a fish's tail!

'Batfish!' I cried, gasping. I picked up the list of runners and stabbed the page frantically. 'That's the name of one of the horses, Batfish! Look, bat's wings, fishes' tail; it'll finish third.'

L.J looked at the form. He looked at the picture. He looked at Bronzo and Bling.

'Oh, roight!' exclaimed Bronzo, a grin spreading across his piercings like a join-the-dots drawing. ''Ere, that's dead clever, that is.'

'Wicked,' agreed Bling, gold teeth a-flashing.

'Woss them others then?' said L.J, pointing to the camel and the horse on wheels.

'Um…' I studied the form, then turned back to my drawing. Could that be a wooden horse? That's it! 'Trojan!' I declared. 'As in wooden horse, the Trojan horse.'

'Yur, s'pose it do look sort of wooden, now you mention it,' said L.J. 'Wodger fink, lads?'

Bronzo and Bling frowned, their heads cocked to one side, like they were in an Art Appreciation Class.

'An' the one in front,' said Bling. 'Who da camel?' All three turned to me expectantly.

'Oh yeah, well that'ssss…' I studied the form, up and down, up and down. Nothing to do with camels, deserts, Arabia…

'Not much use if you can't give us the winner,' growled L.J, impatiently tapping the pencil on the desk. He glanced at the clock. 'Come on, come on…'

Try another approach. 'Perhaps we can go by the colour of the shirt,' I suggested.

'Brown?' said L.J. He looked at the info on colours. 'There's no brown here. You don't know, do you?'

I stared at the picture. 'No.'

'BLEEDIN' USELESS!' yelled L.J, breaking the pencil in two. 'What use are second and third if I ain't got a BLEEDIN' WINNER, eh?'

Bronzo and Bling, prompted by the boss's anger, primed themselves for action again.

'Wait, look!' I cried. 'The jockey…he's not a jockey at all. That's why his hat looks funny; it's not a hat, it's a halo. He's a saint; the horse is St Michael's Mount! And the hump-back; St. Michael's Mount's the winner!'

Slowly, L.J's face went from grim scowl to foul grin. 'Lumme, if he ain't given us a second and third into the bargain!' He slapped Bronzo and Bling on their backs. 'You know what this means lads? We're going for the straight tricast. Come on!'

Fifteen

Twenty minutes later, it was all over. Winner: St Michael's Mount.

Runner-up: Trojan.

2nd runner-up: Batfish.

Because L.J bet on all three horses finishing in that order, it meant that he was able to increase his winnings greatly. So although he only put £20 on the bet, he got back £6,540! Can you believe it? I really was like the goose that laid the golden egg. And now here I was, back in my exam seat with the clock going *glatch*, *glatch*, only now I had less time because the next race was at 2:45 and it was already almost two o'clock. L.J said if it wasn't enough time, just concentrate on the winner.

Perhaps this time he'd place a really big bet, and the police would get interested, I thought. But thinking about the police only got me thinking about Mum and Dad again. I tried to force all that aside, but it kept creeping into my thoughts. Probably because they, no doubt, were thinking about nothing else but me, and I was picking that up and getting my system all clogged.

I studied the names, I tried to draw. I drew a horse, but it was a plain old common-or-garden horse, and I could tell the signals just weren't coming through. Instead I was getting 'Pablo, Pablo, where are you?' My hand moved. And what I drew was this:

'Roight, give it 'ere!' demanded Bronzo, marching in with Bling before I'd barely finished. 'Come on, the race is in twelve minutes, we've gorra bet to make!' He began gathering up all the drawing things.

'No! I'm sorry, it's not—'

'Hey, listen up man,' bellowed Bling, grabbing me by the wrist. 'Da boss needs da goods S.A.P, comprendez?' and he snatched the drawing and bolted for the door. 'Yo,' he added on his way out.

'Need a name, man.'

I couldn't answer, I just shrugged and shook my head.

'Come on,' insisted Bronzo, pulling on Bling's arm. 'We'll figure it out, like.' And off they went.

* * *

Another commercial break. My mind was spinning; I was in big trouble now. I had no idea how much money L.J was going to bet this time, but I suspected that after that first triumph, it would be a lot. And he was going to lose, there was no doubt about that. Well, that wasn't exactly my fault, was it?

Somehow I reckoned he wasn't going to see it that way.

I thought about the drawings; might they be some sort of prediction? It certainly felt that way, but it wasn't at all straightforward. Symbolic, as Dad would have said. You had to work at figuring it out.

I knew even as I was drawing it that the bird bursting into flames was a phoenix; the mythical bird that is always getting re-born out of the ashes of its own funeral pyre. But that was only a small part of the puzzle; it wasn't any old phoenix, but a phoenix with my own mum's head. Sad at first, happy in the end. That had to be good, didn't it? Surely it meant that she had to go through something terrible – i.e. her son's kidnap – but afterwards, everything would be OK. That was one way of reading it. But it was frustrating; I wasn't in the picture, so how could I be sure I'd be returned to her? For all I knew, it might mean that she would go through a terrible time mourning poor Pablo's death, but eventually she'd get over it. I remembered the weeping women in my Shed Drawings; there seemed to be a link, but what I was to make of it, I couldn't tell. Ghosts…a house…a baby… What was it all about?

Oh no, here they come.

I heard the *clink*, *clink* of Bronzo and Bling's assorted metal attachments. The bolts slammed back, they burst in. 'Roight, you!' spat Bronzo. 'You've gorra lot to answer for.'

'I tried to tell you—'

'Mute it, man,' growled Bling, as the two of them grabbed me by the arms and led me upstairs.

Only chinks of daylight streaked in above the closed curtains in L.J's warm, smoky study. He stood behind the desk, hands on hips with his back to us, all sweat-patchy. I was brought to my seat.

He turned sideways, staring at the floor. He was doing that thing with his mouth that teachers sometimes do when they're so OUTRAGED and FURIOUS that they don't know where to begin. Sort of squirming it around like they've got a bit of Mars Bar stuck in their teeth. After a very long time, he looked at me sideways.

I licked my lips, but they were still dry. 'Sir, I didn't mean to—'

'You didn't mean to what?' he interrupted, turning now to face me. Bronzo sat on the desk and glared at me as well, for added effect, picking his teeth with the nail-file attachment on his Swiss Army knife.

'It wasn't …I…'

'Hmm? You didn't mean to what? Mislead me? So what, *hexactly*, was you trying to do, eh?'

'Well, it's just I was having trouble—'

'Not 'alf as much trouble as there's going to be if you don't win that money back for me!' he snapped.

'Tut tut tut,' added Bronzo, shaking his head slowly. He was really enjoying this.

They went all blurry as my eyes began to swim with tears.

'I suppose you didn't *mean* us to think you'd drawn that 'orse called Fireball, is that correct?' said L.J

'No, no I didn't…'

'Ha!' went Bronzo, sneering contemptuously as he chiselled at his crooked, yellow eye tooth.

'And it were some *other* jockey you was on about, not the one called Pigeon, is that correct?'

I almost wanted to laugh. Fireball! Pigeon! Of course! 'No sir, honest!'

'Six. And a. Half. Thousand. Pound,' whispered L.J, then fell silent again. I didn't dare say anything. Was it my fault he was stupid enough to blow all his winnings on a hunch like that? I thought my face would melt, it was so hot.

'SIX ANNA HALF GRAND!' shouted L.J suddenly.

Bronzo leapt two feet in the air, 'AAARGH!' as he stabbed himself in the gum with the nail file. 'OWW!' he howled, clamping his hands to his mouth, the Swiss Army knife now jangling about on its chain.

'OOWWW! I'm bleeding!'

'Oh, fer cryin' out loud!' groaned L.J

Bling burst out laughing, a big stereophonic belly laugh, a real thigh-slapper.

'OOWWW!' howled Bronzo, hopping up and down, chain rattling.

I wiped my eyes – get the knife! I thought. There it was, the clasp within reach, *jangle jangle*, all I had to do was unhook it from the belt. Quick! This was the moment; Bling was crying with laughter, L.J was trying to help Bronzo staunch the flow of blood with Man-Size Kleenexes from the other side of the desk.

I reached over, flipped open the clasp, and off it came. Yes! I gripped it tightly in my right hand and quickly grabbed the Swiss Army knife with my left so it didn't dangle.

Bronzo lunged for Bling, bloody tissues falling everywhere. 'I'll 'ave you, I will!' he threatened, and the two of them began to wrestle.

I crept sideways and around the chair and backed away. I almost tripped on the too-long jeans, which bagged around my shoeless feet. I got to the open doorway, turned and ran into the marble hallway and straight for the front door, hoiking up the jeans as I went.

'Get him!' I heard L.J shout. I pulled on the front door latch, but it stopped partway, a chain holding it at four inches. I turned as they were almost upon me and showed them I had the knife, which made them freeze just long enough for me to turn again and make a dash across the hall for the side-door which I remembered led to the garage. I grabbed the handle, it swung open, and having let go of my jeans for a split-second, my right foot caught in the left leg making me stumble on the steps down to the oily concrete floor, dropping the Swiss Army knife as I spread my hand to break the fall.

'Nice try,' I heard L.J say as Bronzo picked up the knife and Bling grabbed me by the scruff of the neck.

Sixteen

Heathrow airport.

Under different circumstances, I think I'd have been blown away by the place. I've always liked stations, and this was like that, only times ten. OK, first up I should explain that yes, I'm flying somewhere but no, I haven't been rescued. Secondly, no I'm not jumping up and down, screaming, 'Help! I've been kidnapped!' You want to know why? Well they'd thought of that one, hadn't they? L.J carefully explained that something very nasty indeed could happen to my mum and dad if I caused any trouble. Seems he had a whole network of nasty pals dotted around town, and all it would take is one phone call. He'd been having me followed ever since that day at the betting shop and so he knew where my house was. I kept quiet.

So that's how I wound up doing the soft-shoe-shuffle with the package tour brigade, at the Heathrow check-ins. But like I say, I was in no shape to appreciate it. It was almost like I wasn't really there, just watching everything on some great wrap-around telly. That would be the sedative. They made me take this medicine, you see, and it made everything sort of iron out. I just glided along and things happened around me. I expect if a rhinoceros had gone charging through Passport Control I'd have just blinked slowly and gone, 'Oh look, a rhinoceros!' It was very peaceful, actually. Especially after I'd had such a nightmare day. Me and Antonio – that's my minder – we barely said two words to each other. Oh, I should say that L.J and the guys weren't with us. Or rather they were there, and taking the same flight but traveling separately, and pretending they didn't know us. Clever, eh? Oh yeah, they had it all planned out.

Antonio was big and dark and Spanish-looking. And since, according to my passport, I was now no longer Pablo Hobbs, but Pedro del Rio, I had to be dark and Spanish-looking too. That's right, there'd been stuff going on behind the scenes. See, this Antonio was posing as my uncle. Ha! I never had an uncle, always sort of wished I did, and now I was getting a new one every day. Hello Uncle L.J! Hello Uncle Antonio!

And now I was even a real pretend Spanish person, not a phony pretend English one. I should explain about the passport. That's why Bronzo took the photo; straight off, they knew they'd probably be whisking me away to sunny Spain, so they forged me a passport. Dyed my hair black, too. That meant they had to alter the pic because, of course, when they took it I had light brown hair. I wondered about that. Why didn't they dye my hair, then take the picture? But like I say, they thought of everything. I mean, think about it: if they'd have tried to do it the first night, they probably realised I might have put up a bit of a fight. And they couldn't have drugged me then, 'cause it could have affected my predicting abilities. So they did the digital thing on the computer. Bling, it turns out, is a bit of a techie on the sly.

So that's the 'how'. As for the 'why'; well, to put it in L.J's words, he's a gambling man, he knows about odds. And getting me off English soil straight away tipped the odds in his favour when it came to being one step ahead of the law. Plus, in spite of my little piece of 'mischief' (after which I think he felt he'd got me 'tamed') I was still his little goose that laid the golden eggs. You've got one of those, and you choose your lifestyle.

'Lovely place, Spain,' he'd said. 'Gorgeous beaches, gorgeous weather. And yer don't even have to speak Spanish! Ain't that right, Bling?'

'Solid.'

'Lot of mountains in Spain,' L.J went on. 'Beautiful. Sarah Nevada an' all that.'

'Sierra,' said Bling, not looking up from the computer screen. He was in the middle of digitally re-mastering my hair at the time.

'All right, no need to get poncey,' retorted L.J. 'You mind your business, I'll take care o' mine.

110

Where was I? Oh yeah, yer Spanish 'SEA-AREAS'. Cold up there, y'know, on them mountain peaks. Brrr! Wouldn't want to be stuck up there wivout a woolie or five.' He gave a sharp intake of breath. 'Not a lot of life, neither. 'Cept some very hungry wolves. So, like, if you was to get lost up there, could be nasty. How we doin' there, Bling?' He strolled over to the computer and peered at the screen.

'Oh yeah, that's the business. Print it!'

I wasn't saying a lot. I was gagged and tied to the chair, with Bronzo guarding me; this was my reward for trying to escape. And I had gunk on my hair. L.J turned to me and took a long drag on his cigar. He pulled up a chair and straddled it. Blue smoke streamed from his nose as he fixed me with that strange, squinty stare of his.

'So, Pedro. That's your name now. Not too difficult; almost the same, really. You stick with it, understand? Good.' He inspected my hair. 'How we doing with the old barnet, Bronze?'

'Five more minutes, boss, and I'll rinse it out, like.'

'There's service, eh, Pedro? New threads, even a new hairdo into the bargain! See, you're well looked after here. 'Course it works both ways. You don't get something for nothing in this world. Er, that is unless you win the lottery or summink. Or place the right bet on the right horse, ahem! But right now things is not looking too good for you, Pedro.'

'Or inheritance,' interrupted Bronzo. 'If someone dies, like, and leaves you a lorra money. Then you get something for nothing.'

L.J just rolled his eyes, waited for him to finish, then went on. 'See, Pedro we're giving you one last chance to prove your worth. You look after us, we look after you. And right now, you're not ful*filling* your part of the *bargain, ARE YOU?*' He paused as he tried to contain the rage that was turning his face purple, the thought of his lost thousands bringing him to the brink of tears.

'Or if you rob a bank…' said Bronzo.

'SHUT UP!' shouted L.J. He was shaking now. He wagged his finger at me. 'All right Pedro, you listen, and you listen good. I'm only going to say this once. You play the game, you'll be all right. You DON'T play the game, you're out in the cold, understand? I'm talking SIERRA NEVADA for you, up there in the mountains, where no one'll hear you scream!'

*   *   *

So here I was at Heathrow. Yes, there had been an aeroplane in my Shed Drawings, hadn't there? I really had to pay more attention. But it was hard, not having them with me to look at.

The worst part was having airport officials study 'my' passport, then look at me and not see Pablo Hobbs, like I prayed they would, even in my medicated calmness. My eyes implored silently, 'Come on, it's me, Pablo!'

Surely I'd been on the news by now. How could they not see? But they didn't; I was invisible. And there was Antonio at my side, smooth as butter, nodding and taking the documents as they were handed back to him and guiding me with gentle ease, just touching my elbow.

I'd only flown once before, and that was when I was three, so I don't remember it. And because it was late, and because I had chill pill pumping round my veins, I don't remember much about this flight either. I slept nearly the whole way; a blissful nothingness interrupted here and there with a variety pack of vile sensations in assorted parts of my body. First it was the ears: it felt as if I was having injections in both of them, then I thought my head would explode. Antonio gave me a sweet, and that made it better.

You probably know all that stuff about pressure, right? 'Cause if you're anything like most of my mates, you've flown a gazillion times, and it's like, so what? But it was all new to me. I think there were about half a dozen babies on the flight who were having the same thing going on with the ears, and their way of dealing with it was to make sure no one on the plane was going to get off lightly when it came to ear torment. It was the crèche from hell. Next up was the nose; a sweaty smell that reminded me of the school canteen, and I woke to find a tray of astronaut food hovering in front of me. I waved it away and went back to sleep. I could barely open my eyes, let alone eat anything. Not long after that I got the gut torture, because the plane was doing the jumbo jig and playing havoc with my insides. Apparently we were being buffeted around up there like a dinghy being thrashed by fifty-foot waves, but it was Nothing to Worry About, so I didn't worry.

And then there was the balmy Spanish night air and palm trees and then big bright pictures of beaches and mountain villages, and then everything was the same in reverse. Antonio lives in Spain, of course, and he had his van right there ready to go, just like the one that took me to Heathrow. And just like the London journey, I was tied up once I was safely hidden in the back of the van. The drug had worn off by now, and I was awake the whole way. Fat lot of good it did me, though. I knew the airport was at a place called Malaga, but after that I hadn't a clue where we went. Couldn't even time it, although it wasn't that long a drive. Maybe less than an hour. When the van stopped, Antonio took me, still bound, across a courtyard to an empty house that gleamed palely in the moonlight and smelt lovely. My new prison.

Seventeen

Dear Donald,

Thought I'd send you a postcard from Sunny Spain! It's fantastic weather here. The house is really nice, with a terrace and a swimming pool and a lovely garden. And guess what, I got to see an Arsenal match yesterday! You can watch English telly here. Did you see it? I was in heaven.

Three nil! Brilliant.

Wish you were here,
Pablo

It's all true. Except, of course, I never wrote the postcard, let alone sent it. It *was* fantastic weather, and there *was* a pool and a lovely garden. But I only knew this from standing on the toilet and looking through the bars on the window. The downstairs bathroom was the only bit of the house I ever got to see apart from my own basement room. The bathroom had no lock, and when I wanted to go I had to ask Bronzo or Bling, whoever was guarding me at the time, since of course my own room did have a lock – on the outside. And it was damp, damp, damp down there in my room; another boring beige box, another thin, lumpy mattress. The tiny air vent near the ceiling did nothing to air the place out, so the slight smell of mould never left my nostrils, and my clothes never really dried out. I puked a couple of times; Purple Gremlin had grown so large there wasn't space for anything else in my belly. I ate nothing.

Oh, the bit about the match is true, believe it or not. It was a special treat, a reward for a race I predicted. L.J was so happy I was back on form, he let me see the match. OK, I was chained to the couch leg, but still.

Now came the big one. L.J was gearing up to put everything on it, and was looking forward to winning back everything he'd lost, and then some.

Meanwhile I had a plan of my own.

You know I said how they never left me alone with the drawing things? Well I mean *never*. Like I say, pencils could make a nasty weapon, so I wasn't to have them, just like I wasn't ever to have shoes on my feet. But I expect they'd also worked out that if I could predict things, it would give me a definite advantage when it came to things like planning my escape. They let me have tissues, and I tried to figure out a way of drawing on those, but I still had nothing to draw *with*.

Well, ha ha, but whatever else they took away from me, they couldn't take my thoughts. And I had a lot of time for thinking. So in between games with my old friends Joey Sock-face and Ollie Underpants, that's what I did. Lonely it might have been down there, but I didn't allow myself the luxury of being bored; I got really good at thinking. And it was thinking about those Shed Drawings that took up a lot of my time. Page one had already happened; the kidnap, imprisonment, the horses turning into money. So remembering everything from page two was dead important, I'd decided. Not being able to write a list, I had to compose one mentally. What I came up with was this:

aeroplane (check)
mountains
palm trees
figure in empty, dark room (check)
boy running
other running figures
a car (taxi?)
a boat
ghosts (?)
crying women
a baby
a house (with pigeons?)
assorted other scribbles & letters

I figured the mountains and palm trees just meant 'Spain'. At least I hoped so; I shuddered at the thought that I might yet be abandoned in the snowy peaks of the Sierra Nevada. The running boy had to be me, and again I hoped it meant I would escape – although the other running figures might mean I'd be chased and caught again. Cars and boats definitely seemed to indicate travel, but who I'd be traveling with was anybody's guess. Ghosts – well, that was a complete mystery. Halloween? Wrong time of year.

Crying women. I remembered looking at the ones I'd drawn, in those days before I got caught. One of them reminded me of a picture I'd seen in the Picasso book. Picasso painted a lot of crying women, as you can imagine, what with so many of them being madly in love with him, and him being dead mean to them the whole time. He'd lure them into his studio with his big black staring eyes and they were powerless to resist. Then I reckon he'd just go, 'Your nose is too big' or something, and they'd burst into tears. Well, anyway, there had been a crying woman chewing on a hankie, and for some reason she did look vaguely Picasso-ish. There had to be a reason for that, didn't there? I'd have to figure out what that reason was. Well, he was Spanish after all, wasn't he?

OK, lastly, a house and a baby. And some scribbly bits. One or two birds on the house; pigeons or something. I remembered a story I'd read in the Picasso book, about when he was a boy. His dad was a painter too, and painted a lot of pigeons. Picasso was dead useless at school and hated going; he was always pulling a sickie so he'd get to stay home and draw pigeons too. When he was nine, his dad made him sit an exam, and of course he was rubbish. He only passed because he snuck a look at the answers on the teacher's blotter. And when he got home, his way of proving that he'd learnt something was to do pictures of pigeons made up of numbers. That was all numbers were good for as far as he was concerned; shapes to form pictures with. It made me laugh because his dad probably threw his hands up and thought, what am I going to do with him? Whereas *my* dad would have been ecstatic!

I was getting side-tracked. The drawing of the woman had got me thinking about Picasso, and then Picasso's pigeons, which probably had nothing to do with the ones in my house drawing. 'Oh, if only I had the pictures to look at!' I found myself saying aloud.

'Hey, but think about it kid; they got 'em back home,' said a voice.

'Who said that?' I said, turning round. There was Richie Roach, sitting on my bed and munching a mouldy piece of orange rind. 'What are you doing here?'

'Eating garbage. Mmm, good stuff, this.'

'I mean, why are you here?'

Richie picked his teeth. 'You tell me, it was your idea. Guess you could use some company, huh?'

'Well yes…'

'That's right. Gotta have someone to talk things over with, might as well be me. Think of me as being like that little guy sits on your shoulder.'

'What little guy?'

'Didn't you ever hear stories where the person don't know what to do, and he's got a little devil on one shoulder, and a little angel on the other? Well, that person sometimes got to decide which one he's going to listen to.'

'Come to think of it, that does sound familiar. So which are you, devil or angel?'

'How do I know? I'm a cockroach! So, how you gonna get outta this dump?'

I sighed. 'I can't, it's impossible.'

'Y'know, if I had that attitude, I'd 'a killed myself by now, you know that?'

'It's different for you, you're not a prisoner. I mean, that cupboard door, the door to Under-the-Sinksville, is always getting left open. No chance of that ever happening here.'

'Hey, cut it out in there, man!' bellowed Bling from outside the door.

'Ah, take a walk, you piece 'a drek!' Richie called back.

'Ssh!' I hissed, clapping my hand over his mouth. You'll get me into even more trouble than I'm in already!'

'Drek, drek, drek!' taunted Richie the moment my hand was removed.

Thump, thump, thump, went Bling's boot on the door.

'Can it, fruitcake!' He turned up the volume on his radio.

I had my hand over Richie's mouth again. 'What's the big idea?'

Richie yanked my hand away and scuttled up the wall. 'To show you things ain't as bad as you think. And because I like the word 'drek'. Anyhow, point is, you ain't just any old kinda prisoner. You're special. They need you, so they gotta be nice to ya, don't they?'

'"Nice" isn't exactly what I'd call it.'

Richie swallowed the last piece of rotten peel. 'They ain't trying to have you for breakfast, like Gladiator the Cat!'

'Well, I suppose when you put it like that…'

'Exactly. Number two, you got tricks up your sleeve you ain't found yet.'

'What do you mean?'

'I mean you can see into the future,' said Richie, coming back down the wall. 'Hoo-ee! If I could do that, I'd 'a been long gone, you betcha.' He licked his lips and patted his belly. 'You got any more garbage around here?'

'I *can't* see into the future. I can only do it when I'm drawing, and I've nothing to draw with.'

'You still don't get it, do you? Think about it: wasn't so long ago, you didn't know you could do *that*. You know when you was a little kid, you had to read out loud. You couldn't just do it in your head, right? Your mom would say, read this, and reading it meant saying it. Right?'

'How do you know? You're a cartoon cockroach.'

'Hey, don't knock it, kid. I came right outta somebody's imagination! I knows a bit about brains, I was born in one. Point is, there was a time when someone said two add two is what, and little old you'd be countin' your fingers. Then one day you didn't have to any more; two add two, zip, it's there. Answer's four. Well, who's to say, with a bit of practice, you can't do the same with your predicting?'

'You don't understand. It's harder!'

'Harder schmarder. You're older, too. You get better at things. And if you can predict what's going on with old cigar-face and his pals, who knows what you might be able to do. Think about it, kid. Oh, and by the way, the same goes for those pictures you did before you was captured. You gotta think *real* hard about those. I'll see ya 'round.'

Then he was gone. 'Hey, come back!' I called. I got down on the floor and looked under the bed.

I heard the door open. 'What's goin' on 'ere then?' said L.J.

Eighteen

L.J's concern for my mental health was touching. Bling told him I was talking to myself, so he was worried I was losing my mind. And this, of course, was a major big-time worry for him, since the goings-on in my mind were something of very particular interest to him. Wait 'til you hear what he did about it, though; he started getting Bronzo or Bling, whichever of them was on duty, to come into my room now and then, so's we could have conversations. Like that's really going to sort me out!

So Bronzo'll come in and say something like, 'So, how ya doin'?'

And I'll go, 'Great. Fantastic,' in a dead sarcastic tone.

'Lunch alroight?'

'Yep.' (I'd started eating a bit by then.)

'Good.'

Silence for a bit, while Bronzo tries really hard to find a safe subject. Eventually he'll come up with something like, 'Hey, you know what's Spanish for sandwich? Bocadillo.

That's not the sort with two slices of bread, though.'

'A breadless sandwich?'

'No, wor' I mean is, it's a bread roll, like.'

But that's exactly the problem: there is no safe subject. Because then I'll just say, 'Well, thanks for that! Next time I'm out and about and feeling a bit peckish, I'll know what to ask for, won't I?'

And then he winds up all offended, saying, 'Alroight, I'm only making conversation.' It would be hilarious if it weren't so painful.

Oh, I didn't tell you what L.J came to see me about. Well, surprise surprise, it was another race. Only this was to be the biggie; I'd proved once more I could come up with 'the goods' as he put it, so now he was really going to go for gold.

'Don't think you won't be rewarded yerself,' he added. 'You'll do well out of this, Pedro. Very well indeed. *If* you play yer cards right. If yer don't…but I think we talked about the Sierra Nevada before, didn't we? Yeah, that's right. But you'll come up trumps. Won't he, Bling?'

'Yo.'

I won't bore you with the details. Same deal as before; first, second, third, in that order. I did the drawings, I still had it, and yes, I won L.J the money. I don't know how much, but I do know he was putting several thousand on another straight tricast. Doing the sums, it wasn't stretching the imagination too far to think I might have made him a millionaire. So that was good, wasn't it?

No being kicked out of the back of the van at night time on a frozen wolf-infested mountain-top.

I waited for my reward; I did get some chocolate, but so far that was about it. Waiting, waiting…I was doing a lot of that. Waiting to be rescued; no sign of that yet, either. I wondered if anyone had figured out yet that I was in Spain. But how could they?

Then I realised; they had clues. My Shed Drawings!

That mad jumble of pictures and scribbles just might be considered evidence. Because they'd know from Donald that I could predict things, which the pictures proved because they showed me being captured. And while the rest of it could hardly be described as telling a story, they might just have put together aeroplane + mountains + palm trees = me getting flown to Spain.

Ah, who was I kidding? How many parts of the world had mountains and palm trees? And what chance was there that they'd make sense of the rest of it when even I, the artist, couldn't figure it out?

Oh boy. Change the subject; think about rewards. I heard the doorbell ring: hey, maybe it's a present for me! My reward. A Gameboy, perhaps; that would be nice. But no one came downstairs.

There seemed to be a lot going on upstairs lately, for some reason. The phone and the doorbell kept ringing, and there were comings and goings and rattling noises. I asked Bronzo about it, but he wasn't giving anything away.

Then Richie showed up again, this time enjoying a piece of soggy lettuce.

'Did you do it yet?'

'You mean, did I predict anything?'

'Yes!'

'No, I've been busy. Do you know how tiring it is, predicting those races? Well, no, you wouldn't. But it's really hard work, I can tell you; like doing an all day test on stuff you haven't revised. I'm washed out, all I want to do is sleep.'

'Listen kid, you gotta start doing a little detective work if you're gonna get anywhere,' said Richie, a string of slimy lettuce hanging from his mouth like a bogie. 'Like, what's with all the commotion upstairs, huh?'

'I don't know. Bronzo wouldn't tell me,' I whispered. 'And keep your voice down, will you?'

'OK, so *guess*! L.J's just won a stack o'cash. So he could be buying stuff for the house, right?'

'Wrong. It's not his place, it's Antonio's.'

'Good, good. Process of elimination; strike that. Hmm…needs more mayo…'

I wrinkled my nose. 'You're disgusting.'

'Hey, enough with the insults already, I'm helpin' ya here! And I'll have you know, cleaning up garbage is a very environmentally friendly thing to do. Anyways, so what else might you do when you just won somethin', huh kid?'

I shrugged. 'Celebrate, I suppose.'

'Got it in one! Celebrate.' Richie waggled his cockroach brows at me. 'My guess is old cigar-face up there's going to have himself a party.'

'But he lives in England. What's he going to do, fly everyone over?'

'That's for you to figure out. Think about it; this could be your big chance to get away. OK, so let's suppose there's gonna be a party, Next you gotta find out when it is.'

'I don't know; at the weekend I guess.'

'You gotta do better than that, kid. Exercise that predicting muscle. Go to it. So long!'

So long. Why do Americans say that? I suppose they mean, 'I like you so much, it's going to feel *so long* till the next time I see you.' 'Cause time does that, doesn't it? If you're having a great time, it just whizzes by, and vice versa. Like, for me, down in that damp, dank basement with its hard blue tiled floor and its nasty synthetic bedding that slid all over the place, it felt as if I'd been there for, oh, *weeks*. But if I counted the nights, there had been only four of them. That's if I count the first one, when I arrived in the middle of the night and didn't sleep a wink. So that would make this Wednesday evening. Richie was right; even though I felt lousy, I had to force myself to get practising.

If I thought about it really hard, there probably was an instant – a nanosecond – when I knew what I was going to draw before I drew it. Although it didn't start out that way; I remembered at first there was a lot of aimless doodling before I got going, but now…that was it! It was true; I got better at it. I sat up in bed. I stared before me: the room was dimly lit by the tiny chunk of moonlight coming in through the airvent near the ceiling; my only connection to the outside world. I moved to the little desk I used for drawing and sat in the chair, just as if I were about to draw; if I made my brain think that, it might help the images to come through. I even held my right hand the way I would if a pencil were in it. It's like that trick if you need to pee but can't go, and you run the tap. You're playing a little game with your brain, and your brain then sends a message to the part of your body that needs help.

But it was like when you've forgotten someone's name, and it's on the tip of your tongue; little glimpses of the word flicker in your head, then disappear like fireflies. An image started to come into focus, and just when I started to make sense of it, it all dissolved again. Several times I had to get up and walk around, shake it all out and start again. Man, it was frustrating! And yet…there was something trying to come through, I could *taste* it…Keep at it, I told myself.

I don't know how long I carried on like that; at one point I think I was practically in a trance.

But slowly the pictures started forming properly in my head, and it was exactly the same feeling I'd had every time I'd made a prediction. These weren't just any old images; I knew they were real, they were going to happen.

And that's when the Purple Gremlin woke up and started kicking around in my gut again.

Because no matter what I did, whether I fast-forwarded to the next bit or what, all I got were images of death.

I saw Jesus on the cross. I saw men in black carrying a flower-strewn coffin on their shoulders. I saw candles, I saw faces with tears streaming down their cheeks – there were those weeping women again. I even got some of those weird ghosty figures as well, just like before. It was a funeral, it had to be. How could it possibly be anything else?

There was one possible explanation; perhaps it wasn't mine. I knocked on the door. 'Bronzo?'

'Yeah?'

'I need to ask you something.'

Bronzo unlocked the door and opened it a little way.

'Worr is it?'

'Did someone die?'

The blank look told me all I needed to know. 'Worr, you mean killed, like?'

'I just mean died. Croaked. Kicked the bucket.'

'No. Why'd you ask?'

I shivered. 'I didn't know if…maybe there was going to be a funeral.'

'Funeral? Worra you on about?'

Nineteen

So that was it, then: I was dying. I couldn't get warm that night, and I lay awake for ages, shivering. I had a sore throat and an earache. In the morning I couldn't wake up. I'd half-wake, think about getting up, then fall back to sleep again. And now I was hot, and dreaming crazy stuff. Things from my drawings were in there – the ghosts, the crying women, babies in boats, all joining the funeral procession. Then it all changed, and now there was daylight, and a feeling of gut-wrenching terror – I don't know what else. When I woke up I had drool all over my pillow and my GOAL! pyjamas were drenched in sweat. Bling stood over me. 'Hey man, chill. You is delirious!'

I asked for a doctor, and he went and got L.J.

'He's feverish, innit,' Bling told him. 'Talkin' like a crazy guy.'

L.J felt my forehead. 'Ah, a few Lemsips, you'll be right as rain in a day or two.'

'But it's so damp in here,' I protested. 'I think I've got pneumonia.'

L.J felt the wall. 'Bling, get us one of them space heaters from upstairs, will you? That'll dry it out nice. And get the lad an extra blanket.'

'No, I want to go outside! You said I'd be rewarded for winning you all that money. Well, I want sunshine, that's what I want for my reward.'

'Oi!' snapped L.J, clutching my pyjama shirt and thrusting his red-veined nose up to mine. 'We'll 'ave none of that!' he growled. Those eyes close up freaked me out; one bloodshot, the other not. Blank, glassy stare.

'Did you hear me say anything about you choosing your reward?' he went on. 'No! I'm in charge around here, and I'll say what you get fer your reward and when. Understand?' He let go, and I flopped back onto the bed.

'But I'm ill!'

'Look, you ain't got pneumonia, all right?' yelled L.J. ''S a cold, that's all. Bling'll get you that heater.'

Out he went, but the glassy stare stayed with me.

Bling came in a few minutes later with the heater, the blanket and the Lemsip.

I planned my question carefully, since it was clear I wasn't supposed to know about any party.

'Bling?'

'Yeah?'

'L.J likes it in Spain, doesn't he?'

'What's it to you, man?'

'Just…making conversation.'

Bling folded his arms. 'Da boss is cool with it, man. But you knew that.'

'Yeah I know, it's just…I wondered if maybe he comes here a lot?'

'Get to the point.'

'Well, it's just, I suppose if he's been coming here a lot, you know, for a long time, he'd know quite a lot of people here, wouldn't he?'

Bling eyed me suspiciously. 'Maybe he do, maybe he don't. That all?'

I paused. 'Yes…no, wait.'

Bling sighed sarcastically and made an exaggerated 'waiting' pose.

'You know you said I was…talking in my sleep?'

'Yeah.'

'What was I saying?'

'Dumb stuff. Talking 'bout 'Santa', like you thunk it was Christmas.' He laughed sneeringly. 'Lickle boy wants his pressies! An' you kept goin', "casa, casa!" Didn't know you spoke Spanish, man.'

'It's Spanish?'

'Yeah, Spanish for 'house', innit. Everyone knows that. Drink your drink, man, you is losin' it.'

Santa…casa…what could I have been on about? I must have been dreaming, but I couldn't remember a thing. I slept some more, then for lunch I had a cup of chicken broth and a bocadillo. After that I felt a little stronger, well enough to take a shower. When I was drying myself, I could hear L.J out on the terrace, talking on the telephone. I stood on the toilet, to get a better listen as he paced around the pool.

'Yur, reckon there'll be about forty-odd…is that all right, mate?…oh, Wayne's runnin' it, is he? That's good, you don't have to shut up shop then…haha!…she coming too?…Excellent, excellent, I'll pay you extra…'

Bling rapped at the door with his rings, making me jump. 'Yo, Pedro. Vamoose.'

I didn't say anything, in case L.J heard me.

'…So we on for the barbecue?' he went on. 'Fantastic…oh, you got them Spanish sausages? I like them, yur…great…great…OK seeya mate. 'til tomorrow.'

Bling burst in; I quickly jumped off the toilet. 'No spyin', man!' he barked.

'I…I wasn't, I was just…'

Bling flung me my jeans. 'Get outta here!'

* * *

Back in my room, I had time to think. Acres of time. Tomorrow, barbecue party. That's what I had to concentrate on; and forget all about the funeral for the time being. I'd done quite enough thinking about that as it was, anyway, and decided it was only making me iller. I even got quite angry about it. Who was running my life anyway? Didn't I have a say in whether I lived or died?

Surely it was possible to have some control over it. Take horoscopes (or should that be horror-scopes?) The people that write them have to say things like:

Libra: Try not to allow yourself to become too distracted.

Because if they wrote:

Libra: On Friday afternoon you will be distracted when crossing the road, and you will be run over and killed by a bus — well, that couldn't be true of all Librans, could it? Which must mean that even though the stars are working behind the scenes, you are still the main player on the stage. I don't know what this says about the horses and riders in all those races, but I decided not to worry about that for the time being.

Barbecue. Tomorrow. That much I knew; I had to concentrate on that and nothing else. I sat at my desk and thought hard, and eventually – more quickly this time – the pictures started coming through. I saw cars arriving; daytime still, but the sun low in the sky. Buckets of iced water, people pulling bottles from them. Suntanned men and women. No kids. Smoke rising from the barbecue. More bottles being opened. Sun going down.

Dancing inside the house. A woman in a red dress. Some random stuff crept in there at this point; bugs, butterflies, Richie Roach…come on, *focus!* But it was no good, I had to stop; this was very hard. I took a break, walked around and took some deep breaths, then sat down and concentrated again.

Now I was getting L.J and Antonio talking to each other – no, *shouting*. Lots of arm-waving, and now Antonio takes hold of the front of L.J's shirt and shoves him up against the wall. People back off; L.J gets away, but Antonio punches him and he falls, knocking over a small table and sending glasses and bottles crashing to the ground. Now they're both on the floor, fighting. Another person seems to be trying to break it up, but the fight goes on. I just got a glimpse of Bling, before it all went dark again.

I got up and walked around again. A fight! And if Bronzo or Bling or both of them got involved in trying to break it up, that could mean a great opportunity for me to get away. Two things I needed to know:

(1) Who would be on guard duty that night? (Easy to find out.)

and

(2) What time would the fight happen? (Not so easy.)

Yes, I couldn't very well go to Bling and say, 'Hey, I hear L.J's going to get in a fight with Antonio tomorrow night; what time will it be please?' I would have to try and predict it, but I was already worn out and starting to feel ill again, so I went back to bed. If I was going to run away tomorrow night, I'd need all the strength I could get.

Twenty

Richie visited me again that night.

'So there's going to be a fight, huh?'

'It looks like it.'

'Fightin' over money, I guess. Humans! When will they learn? Brings nothin' but misery.'

'You can talk! You're the richest cockroach in the world. You're on pencil cases and T-shirts all over the place. You're famous.'

'Hey, I didn't ask to be! You done with that drink, by the way?' he asked, indicating the tiny bit of flat Coke left in a glass by the bed. I waved him on. 'Anyways,' he went on, sipping noisily from the straw, 'it ain't me gets the money...*shlurrp!*...it's the guy who invented me, and the studios who asked the guy to invent me. I'm like you; I may be the star, but they's the ones rolling in it. Welcome to it, too...*shlurrp!*...nothin' but misery. So, you gonna escape?'

'I don't know. Bronzo's on duty, I worked that out. If

only I knew exactly when the fight was going to be, I'd ask to go to the loo right before. That's the only thing they let me out of here for. But trying to find out what time…it's impossible!'

'No it ain't! OK, so you saw stuff that was goin' on at the party, yeah?'

'Yes. Eating, drinking, dancing. So?'

'You gotta zoom in, kid. Hey, who knows, maybe you could even zoom in on the guy's watch, I don't know…*shlurrp!*…point is, there's gotta be clues in there someplace.'

'It's not like having a camera, I can't just "zoom in"!'

Richie wiped his mouth and made a satisfied little 'ahh!' sound. 'Well, you're going to have to figure it out somehow. You can't back out now, kid. So long!'

Man, that cockroach was getting annoying. Especially since I knew he was right. Anyway, before I knew it, the day of the party had arrived and I still had no idea when the fight would be. I must have slept for fourteen hours solid, but when I finally woke up I felt a lot stronger. I still had a sore throat, but the fever had gone. Now it was late afternoon and here's the only clues I had: the woman in red dancing, the bugs, butterflies, and my old pal Richie Roach for whatever reason. I had decided by now that these images weren't random; it felt as if they meant something. The question was, *what*?

I tried to spy on things from the bathroom window, but someone had plonked a whopping great cactus plant slap bang in front of it. Ooh yes, and we know why, don't we? Plus they'd locked the window so there wasn't going to be any yelling 'help!' and getting rescued. So all I got were glimpses of people's legs between the prickly pears. I caught a flash of red skirt; aha! The woman in red. I heard her laugh; a loud shriek, YEE-HEE-HEE!! Like someone had put ice cubes down her dress. She stepped forward and there was clue number two; the butterfly. A butterfly tattoo on her ankle.

'Come on,' called Bronzo from behind the bathroom door.

I jumped down. 'Coming!'

So what was it about the woman in red? Perhaps L.J and Antonio were fighting over her? Then there was Richie…it was a puzzle, all right.

Darkness fell outside the airvent in my cell. The door opened and party noises spilled into the room; it was Bronzo with my supper. I noticed his movements were sort of exaggerated. As he put down the tray he burped. I was close enough to smell the beer on his breath. Brilliant! Bronzo was getting drunk!

He left. I chewed my blackened Spanish sausage and listened. Muffled voices and footsteps, music in the background. The dancing didn't seem to have started yet. Every now and then there was a loud laugh, mostly the YEE-HEE-HEE!! of the woman in red.

I sat at my desk and concentrated on what she and her butterfly tattoo might get up to next. Was she going to dance with Antonio or L.J? No, that wasn't coming through; I saw her dancing alone. Then I saw her fussing around with a pile of CDs and finding the one she wanted. She holds it up and waves it about. Then I get this image of Richie Roach again; what was this with Richie Roach? Were they all going to sit down and watch cartoons? Anyway, right after Richie, that's when the fighting starts. Richie was my cue to get out of there.

Later. The joint was jumping now, the music and the thud, thud above my head much louder. And shouts, whoops and YEE-HEE-HEE's!! Then I heard it, loud and clear: Richie! I want Richie! Or was it 'Ricky'? I jumped up; my signal. *This* was why I had drawn Richie Roach. I held on, just to be sure. Time it badly and it could all go pear-shaped.

Then I heard, "yay! Ricky!" It *was* Ricky; the woman in red had found her man. Or perhaps it was a CD? A new song came on, fast rhythm, pounding beat. Now.

Knock knock. 'Bronzo? I need the toilet.' Bronzo unlocked the door.

I went to the loo. I washed my hands. Any moment now…I kept the tap running. 'Just going to brush my teeth!' I called out. I brushed my teeth. The music went on; still no sounds of any fight.

'Roight, you've been in there long enough, I'm coming in!' called Bronzo.

'No, wait - I'll be right out!'

'You're up to no good,' said Bronzo, barging in. 'Gerr

outta there, you—'

A muffled CRASH!! from above. Bronzo froze, a state of beer-fruzzled alarm working its way across his studded, sweaty face. The shouts and screeches upstairs told me this was the moment I'd been waiting for.

Bronzo lurched around. 'What the—'

From where I stood on the toilet, I threw my towel on him and made a dash for it. There was another door at the top of the stairs, bolted; I yanked the bolt aside. Now Bronzo was closing in on me; in a second I was on the other side of the door and I whumped him with it as hard as I could. I scrambled up more marble stairs into the dark, loud room and from the corner of my eye I saw a blood-stained L.J wrestling with Antonio, a flash of red dress, of Bling's jewellery. More yelling and screeching, partygoers trying to intervene in the brawl. I made a bee-line for the door and I was out in the balmy Spanish night.

Twenty-One

I ran in my bare feet down some steps, past the parked cars and out into the dead-end road. I heard the van engine start up; news was out. I dashed across the road where there was an unfinished building and managed to duck down behind a wall just seconds before the headlights flashed by. I waited. No other cars; there was a fight to take care of. I waited some more; let them get far away.

When all was clear I started walking. I didn't exactly have a plan at this point, but right now I was too busy touching trees and taking great gulps of delicious flower-scented air to notice. Freedom! I jumped and skipped, I did a somersault. And I was completely bowled over by all that *sky*: so much of it! So sparkling! They didn't have sky like that back where I was from.

There was a glow on the horizon and the distant sound of traffic. Before long I had reached the busy main highway, and a group of people were coming towards me and talking REALLY LOUDLY – in English. Panic hit me, until it became clear they were nothing to do with L.J and didn't even notice me. Blimey! What was it with all the English people? Was I really in Spain, or just some sunny bit of England with palm trees and bocadillos and speecy spicy sausages?

It occurred to me to ask them for help, but then I realized that these very red, very ugly people weren't walking straight; they were as drunk as skunks. I decided to cross the road to get away from them. WHOOM! WHOOM! went the cars, non-stop. Finally all seemed clear so I started to cross, but suddenly there was a *HONNNKKK!* as a truck came thundering at me from the opposite direction and I jumped back on the kerb, colliding with the red English people.

'Outta the way, gyppo!' growled a shiny-faced blond man, shoving me. Shaken, I ran across the road, dodging the traffic and getting seriously honked at as the traffic swerved out of my way. I ran and ran and didn't stop until I reached the shelter of some buildings. I leaned against the wall of a darkened furniture showroom and slid to the ground, panting heavily. Blimey, I'd nearly been run over! I'd forgotten that they drove on the other side of the road over here. Perhaps I really was in Spain, after all.

And what was that the man had called me? 'Gyppo'? He'd thought I was a gypsy! This was a new one. Gypsy. I rolled the word over in my mind, wallowing in the exoticness of it. And even though the blond man had been so horrible – could have killed me! – I found that the idea gave me a little thrill. It took me back to when I was four, and the way it felt to be Tarzan. The freedom of it! Right now I felt very, very free, and that could either be scary or exciting. I decided I'd been scared for quite long enough, so I plumped for 'exciting'. And what could be more exciting and exotic than to be a gypsy fortune-teller? Just think what I could do with that! Hey everybody, look at me, I'm…

Pedro the Gypsy Fortune-Teller!

He's wild. He wanders the streets of Spain, living off his wits. The Big Bad Englishmen are hunting him down, but he's too sharp for them! See him dice with death as he dodges the dangerous Spanish drivers!

Marvel at his ingenuity (cue castanets, Spanish guitar) in the bull-ring as the famous matador calls on him in his hour of need. The bull is ferocious, the matador is saying his prayers. 'Bring me Pedro!' he cries, and whoosh, Pedro to the rescue!

He whispers in the matador's ear; 'The bull's been cut, his right eye's going blind. In exactly two and a half minutes' time the eye will pack up. Then he'll charge at you in a northeasterly direction at fifty kilometres an hour – jump to the right, he won't see you!'

Adios, Olé! Pedro saves the day!

Well, right now Pedro's mouth was dryer than the Costa del Very Dry Things, so I visited the very stinky loo in a roadside café, and drank some water from the tap.

No one took any notice of me; I'd never felt so invisible. I thought about asking a customer for money, but then a taxi pulled up outside, and I had a better idea.

'A taxi driver!' thought Pedro, in a flash of inspiration. 'He'll get me out of here!'

Then Pedro remembered he was really Pablo Hobbs from London, England, who not only had no money for a fare, but couldn't earn it by telling the man's fortune either, since he didn't speak Spanish. Still, there were always pictures…

The taxi driver was small and shiny and shaped like a bowling ball. His shirt buttons strained across his belly, and out the top grew a thicket of chest-hair. He hitched up his trousers and sat down at an outdoor table in that Humpty-Dumpty way that very round people have to do in order to balance themselves. He lit a cigarette and spoke to the waitress. While she was serving him, I pinched a stack of napkins and a pen from the counter. If I got near enough, I could pick up his vibes and draw his fortune for him. I went and sat on the ground near his table. He didn't even glance at me. Well, I'd better have some good news for him; it was only going to work if it was something he wanted to hear. I held my pen poised over my napkin and concentrated. I found myself drawing a cat running into the road and getting flattened. Oh no, this wouldn't do at all.

Try again. Another cat, very fat this time. No, no, stop it with the cats! Concentrate. Fat cat gives birth to seven kittens. Urgh! When I looked up again I realised why: a family of stray cats were doing the fandango around the taxi driver's table, as his bread and meatballs had arrived. And since I was on the ground I was nearer to them than to him; I was seeing *their* futures.

I had to focus: I snuck a good look at him, and started again. I saw him driving; OK, no big surprises there. I'd have to try and see the bigger picture; not just the next few hours, but weeks, months – even a year ahead. It wasn't easy.

I saw him eating; ho hum.

I saw him looking at pictures of women in magazines…ahem.

Driving again. Yawn.

I saw him sitting alone in a bar; boy, this guy had a boring life. Ah, but that was the point, wasn't it? Old Humpty here was *lonely*. I looked up; he wiped his mouth with his napkin and lit up another cigarette. Poor guy; I felt sorry for him.

Better find something interesting soon; he might not be here much longer. Ah, at last, this looked promising; a large woman with long black hair, getting off a plane. I saw her cutting someone's hair, sweeping the floor. I saw her outside a shop with a sign that said DOLORES. And I saw her with the taxi driver.

Mr Humpty got up to leave. I jumped up; 'Señor!' I cried, in my best Spanish. He flipped a coin at me and carried on.

'No, no señor! I mean thank you, gracias, but look! I have something to show you.' I waved the napkins at him.

He stared at me, cigarette hanging off his lip. 'Inglés?'

'Pictures, look! It's *you*, señor! I tell your fortune.'

He took the cigarette from his mouth. 'I say, you Eengleesh?'

'Si, Señor, yes. You speak English?'

He peered at me sideways. 'No esta gitano?'

I stared at him blankly. 'English. No understand, señor. But I can tell your fortune…er, fortuna?'

The taxi driver raised his eyebrows. 'Ah, ees cigarette you wan', eh?' He jostled the cigarettes at me, which I noticed were called 'Fortuna'.

I shook my head vigorously. 'No, no, no! Look, here,' I insisted, jabbing a finger at the napkins. 'I think you'll find it interesting, interesante; it's about Dolores.'

Smoke streamed from his nostrils like a cartoon bull's steaming breath. 'Dolores!' he cried. 'La conoses, you know her?'

'No, señor. Just look at the pictures.'

He took the napkins and studied them. 'Ay!' he sighed, clapping his hand to his sweaty, hairy chest. 'Dolores, mi amor Dolores! Ella regresa, she come back?'

'Si señor! Yes! I tell your fortune.'

'Ah, entiendo!' said Mr Humpty, at last understanding. 'Sí, fortuna…ahh, Dolores mi amor!' He kissed the napkin. Then he reached into his pocket and beckoned me over. He tried to cram a small wad of euros into my hand.

'No, señor, I need your help. The taxi,' I said, pointing. 'You take me, yes? In taxi, away from here. Er, por favor?'

'You wan' taxi ride? Dondé, where you go?'

'Away!' I cried. 'To…to Malaga. Yes, that's it.' Get to the nearest town, I thought; then find a police station, and I'd be safe at last.

Mr Humpty shrugged, taking a last puff. 'OK, I do.' He threw his cigarette end down and ground it with his shoe, giving me another curious look. 'Incréible.'

At that moment, a large white van shrieked into the forecourt, dust billowing around it. I could just make out two guys inside, and in a flash I knew who it was. 'Help!' I cried, grabbing Mr Humpty's arm. 'It's them, quick!'

Twenty-Two

I dashed to the taxi; Humpty waddled behind, stuffing the napkins in his pocket, Bronzo and Bling behind him, going about ten million times faster. I jumped in the driver's seat, and I don't know why, but I blasted Humpty's horn real loud. (What was I thinking? That the two thugs would be scared off? 'Ooh, aah a loud noise, oh no!' cringe, cringe). Anyway, I'm glad I did, because the ones it did scare were the small, mangey feline kind who at that moment were scavanging around the bins nearby. They shot across the forecourt like their tails were on fire, right in the path of Bronzo and Bling, tripping them up beautifully. I couldn't have designed it better if I were animating the scene. I threw myself into the passenger seat, just as Humpty made it into the car, and we squealed out into the road.

I squinted out the back window as the van's headlights closed in on us, blindingly bright. Humpty rammed his foot down and we surged forward. As we rounded a bend, he overtook two cars and only just made it back into the right lane before a stonking great truck came the other way.

'Mi Dios! You do something bad, hey niño?'

'No, no, it's them! They're my kidnappers, uh, they steal me, you understand?'

'Steal? Steal, what is 'steal'?'

The blinding headlights were right behind us again. 'Oh!' I whimpered. 'Get me to the police!'

'Policía? Is OK, yo no se lo digo, I no tell.'

'No, you don't understand!' But my voice was drowned out by a loud honk as we swerved to overtake another car.

Humpty floored it, but just as I thought we'd shaken them off, there came those dazzling headlights again, and Humpty had to adjust his rear-view mirror so as not to be blinded.

'Oh faster, faster!' I cried, because apart from anything else, I figured a high-speed car chase was *supposed* to grab the attention of the *cops*, wasn't it? I hoped and prayed for the whine of a police siren, but where were they all; in bed? And it was all so frantic, I didn't dare try and explain to el Humptio that I *wanted* the police, I wasn't wanted *by* them, because if I distracted him we might all end up as extra-chunky road salsa.

Then we hit a traffic jam. They weren't directly behind us, but I knew they couldn't be far behind.

'Ay!' said Humpty. 'Semana Santa, how you say? The Week of Holy. Viernes Santo, is, eh…Holy Friday.'

'Good Friday?' Of course, it was Easter weekend. With all the excitement, I'd forgotten to notice I was missing my choccy egg. What that had to do with the traffic jam I had no idea, but there was no time to discuss it now; I was a sitting duck.

'You must get out, niño. Es peligroso, is danger – corre, RUN!'

I reached for the handle. 'Thank you, señor. Muchas gracias.'

'Anda, go!' he said, patting me on the arm. 'Que dios te proteje, God bless you.' He stuffed the wad of euros into my hand. 'Gracias, amigo. I find Dolores, me caso, she shall be…how you say, my wife!'

I pocketed the money, got out of the cab and ran along the middle of the divided highway. Boy, there was certainly something going on! What was that he'd said; Semana Santa? Santa…there was that word again. The traffic wasn't moving, and the streets were filled with crowds of people. I had no idea whether Bronzo or Bling – or both – were following me, but I just kept running, running, although my feet were raw with blisters. I crossed the road and came to a traffic cop at the junction, standing amid the traffic, his whistle piercing the air as he ushered the crawling drivers along.

I tugged his sleeve. 'Por favor, señor?'

He turned and glared at me. 'Fuera! Estoy occupado!'

'But sir...' At that moment I heard a commotion behind me; I glanced back and there were Bronzo and Bling, now on foot themselves and pushing past some angry Spaniards. I dashed across the square and made it to a side street; this was better, more crowded, I just wanted to lose myself in that crowd. But as I went on, the crowd became denser and denser until I found I was stuck in a people jam. I felt a hand on my back and my heart did a somersault; then I turned and saw it was a tiny old lady, pushing her way through. She didn't look at me, just forced me on with her bony little fingers, her shriveled-pumpkin face straining upward as if to get a good view of something. All the faces around me were doing the same thing, and there was a faint thrumming that sounded like drums.

I had to get past this somehow; it freaked me out being stuck wedged between la Pumpkina here and the entire population of Malaga. Not to mention my poor, blistered feet, being squished by Spanish heels every five seconds. It didn't help that I had used up my entire Spanish vocabulary on, 'Please, thank you, mister' and hadn't a clue how you said, 'Excuse me'. So I wriggled and ducked and dived, saying stupid things like, 'Sorry!' and 'Excusez-moi'.

Parrum, parrum, parrum-pom-pom. The drums were louder, and now they were joined by the blare of trumpets or bugles, lots of them by the sound of it.

By crouching low, I was able to weasel my way through the forest of legs, till I came to the very front of the crowd. Now I could go no further, as I had reached the spectacle they were all straining to get a look at.

Twenty-Two

The drummers had arrived, *parrum-pom-pom*, marching slowly in fancy military get-up, all epaulettes, tassels and shiny, feathered helmets. A little boy next to me sat on the edge of the pavement, banging his own little drum and squealing excitedly. Behind the drummers were the buglers. I peered to my left, along the row of adult legs and small children; I figured I might be able to dash past them, keeping low. That way I could get to the back end of the procession and across the street. I went for it, and I wasn't popular, I can tell you. Dirty looks and Spanish cusses from all sides, but I kept on going.

Trouble was, the procession kept on going too; there was just more and more of it, row upon row of shiny shoes and gold piping. And it was all around me and inside me, the brassy braying of the bugles and the pounding of the drums jangling my already nervous bones.

What I saw next made me stop dead in my tracks. The last of the buglers passed by, but this was not the end of the procession. Now came figures in long white robes, like choir singers, except that on their heads they wore these unbelievable black hoods like church steeples, each one must have been more than a metre tall. They covered their faces completely, with just holes for the eyes. My ghosts! Not ghosts at all, as it turned out. One of them led the way, swinging an incence burner and filling the air with its smoky perfume. The others carried big candles on long fancy poles. But it was what was coming up behind them that really got me: a huge life-size Jesus on the cross. Now it all began to make sense; this was the procession I had foretold back in my cell – the one I had thought was a funeral!

The candle-lit Jesus was high, high up, glowing full-colour against the black sky. As he came nearer, I saw Mary at the base of the cross, and the whole thing was mounted on some sort of gigantic carnival float. Only this wasn't on wheels, but supported on the shoulders of dozens of men, like pallbearers at a funeral. The float – no, you couldn't call it a float; think of the fanciest cathedral you ever got dragged round by your parents. Well, imagine that inside out, and you'll have some idea. Above the huge beams which rested on the men's shoulders was an enormous gilded altar with hundreds of deep pink flowers spilling round the sides. Gilt lanterns like fairytale street lamps rose up at each corner and at the back end stood the cross, Mary and Jesus. Still the drums pounded, *parrum, parrum, parrum-pom-pom*; the whole golden galleon sailed on, swaying from side to side as if at sea, furniture wobbling and tinkling as it went. Boy, they really went in for Easter in a big way over here! I'd never seen anything like it.

Now it was passing right by me, sending out a wave of applause like the wake of a ship. Whether the clapping was meant for Jesus, or the men carrying him, or just the stonking great splendiferousness of the whole thing, I neither knew nor cared. I was so relieved, I clapped along with them. Because this wasn't my funeral. Hurray, everybody, I'm not about to die! Then I had to watch it, because I think I got a bit carried away with the happy stuff, and I got a stern look from another old granny. Oops, wait a minute, this is the death of Jesus we're on about here, it doesn't exactly do to go jumping for joy. Better move on.

Well, believe it or not, even that wasn't the end of the procession. Behind Jesus there came another crew of pointy-hats, and beyond them, the stately barge of the Virgin Mary, crowned and robed like a bride or a queen and lit by a hundred candles. Then a bell sounded, and the parade came to a halt. A girl pushed past me and rushed up to a pointy-hat, thrusting forward what looked like tennis ball made of wax. The pointy-hat lowered his pole to allow the candle drip onto the ball, and the girl gleefully rolled it around, not caring about the crimson drips of hot wax, like tears of blood, that fell on her fingers. If only real pain and sorrow could be packaged up like that, I thought. Rolled up and thrown away. Up and down the procession, other children were doing the same, collecting wax. One had a ball the size of a small cabbage; that must have taken an awful lot of wax. I saw the kids' eager, glowing faces like angels. So content and happy were their lives, that they could busy themselves with something so aimless. I envied them.

A stirring in the crowd behind me jolted me back into reality, and I dashed past the pointy-hats and the kids, across to the other side. I glanced back, but there was no Bronzo or Bling; only another boy coming forward. The crowd on the other side of the street obligingly swallowed me up, and I kept on pushing my way through until at last I could breathe the scented night air. I felt a bit like Moses shaking off the Pharaoh's men; I heaved a sigh of relief. Except unlike Pharaoh's lot, Bronzo and Bling wouldn't be drowned in the sea of people behind me, only thrown off course.

Pedro the gypsy fortune-teller, beware! You may have reached the other side, but you're not in the land of angels yet. It's still purgatory.

Oh, stop it with the gypsy fortune-teller thing! I didn't want to be a gypsy any more. I wanted to be like the wax-ball kids, all sinking their heads happily on their soft, fluffy pillows tonight as their mums and dads whisper '*buenas noches*' and turn out the lights.

And again I felt that sickening ache, wanting Mum, wanting a Chinese takeaway in my belly, a hamster concerto on the airwaves, and turpentine in the air.

I kept going, heading down another side street, the drums and bugles growing fainter behind me.

Here the crowd was looser, people in straggly groups going this way and that, and spilling out of cafés. This was better; get far from the parade which traps you in one place. And perhaps I would find a policeman who wasn't so *occupado*, one who might at last help me to get home. Every now and then, I'd see more of the hooded guys, apparently off-duty. They wore different coloured robes; some were purple, and I saw red ones as well. They looked funny, chatting and smoking cigarettes, holding their headgear under one arm; so normal instead of spooky and Halloweeny, as they had seemed before.

Others, their hoods on, walked purposefully as if they were about to join the procession. So I thought nothing of it when two red-robed figures loomed either side of me, until they each grabbed one of my arms, and I heard Bronzo's muffled voice say, 'You've had it now, mate.'

Twenty-Three

'You try anything on now and you're dead, d'ya hear?'

The three of us walked together, Bronzo and Bling in their Easter outfits from God knows where, and me in the middle, my elbows in their vice-like grip. No one gave us a second glance; with their hands hidden under the drapery of their sleeves, it probably looked as if we were just linking arms in a normal, friendly way. I thought about kicking and screaming, 'HELP!' at the top of my lungs. As if he had read my mind, Bronzo growled, 'And don't think you can go yellin' for help, it won't work.'

With the hoods, and the noises all around, it wasn't too easy to catch every word that was said, but I got the gist. And the news was bad. '...Man's right, bro', said Bling. 'Think you can...da police? Think again...Know what you done, man.'

'Me?' I cried. 'I've done nothing wrong!'

A sarcastic laugh came from inside Bling's hood. 'Dat's

what you think. But…little tip-off, innit? …big trouble with them, man.'

'Big trubbs,' added Bronzo. I could just imagine the gloating grin on his face right now.

My face grew hot. 'You're lying! I'm completely innocent, and you know it.'

'Ah,' said Bling. '…Your word against Antonio's, innit?…Man with connections…he told his mate down the comisaría…you stole money off of him. We all know who *he's* gonna believe! Heh, heh!'

'Yeah,' added Bronzo tauntingly. ''Specially when there's a 2,000 euro reward involved, like. Yer can't argue with that!'

So that was it: Antonio's corrupt police friend gets paid handsomely if he can catch young Pedro the 'thief'. Bingo. What L.J would call a win-win situation, 'cause he gets to benefit from a police search, without getting into trouble with them for the small matter of a kidnap. Plus, he knows I won't squeal. 2,000 euros was a small price to pay, after all I'd won for him.

But there was one thing that didn't fit. 'Wait a minute,' I said. 'Antonio and L.J fell out; they were practically killing each other back there!'

The two of them laughed. 'What, that?' said Bling.

'They was just arguin', innit! `S all forgotten now.'

'They both want you back, like,' added Bronzo.

Ay caray! Our hero Pedro is in a real fix now! How is he going to get out of this one?

159

Oh go away, you annoying narrator. Real lives don't have narrators. And narrators never help, do they? They just sit there when the hero's in trouble and do nothing to intervene.

What can he do, our brave little gypsy fortune-teller? Could this be his moment of doom?

See what I mean? Just lets it all happen.

'Couldn't agree with ya more, kid!' said Richie, apparently reading my mind. He was sitting on a nearby food stall, dolloping salsa on a baked potato. 'Happens to me all the time. But hey! Don't forget you got supernatural powers! These guys don't. You gotta *use* 'em, kid. Go for it!'

OK, OK, but how?

He has a mind at least, Wenda, came Dad's voice from somewhere. *All is not quite lost.*

All right, concentrate. Concentrate on the next few minutes. But my mind was a blank; I was panic-stricken. Now we were entering a wide, tree-lined avenue, and the music was louder again. The whole avenue seemed to have been set up like a great, long stadium, with banks of seats filled to overflowing. Over the tops of people's heads, I could just see Jesus sailing forth. Between the shops and cafés on one side, and the stadium seating on the other, was a long line of stalls selling toys, candy floss, baked potatoes and, for some reason, lemons.

'Psst, kid!' said Richie. Now he was on the lemon stall, sprinkling salt on a peeled lemon.

160

'Oh, not you again. Go away, you're no help.'

'Shurrup, yer nutter,' hissed Bronzo under his hood.

'No, kid, listen! I got an idea. Remember that episode when I tripped up Gladiator by emptying the sack o' potatoes all over the floor? Well...' he gestured to the pile of lemons.

I groaned. 'That is such a cliché. And it wouldn't work anyway; it's the sort of thing that only works in cartoons. Leave me alone.'

'Hey, listen up, man!' snapped Bling. 'Can it, you hear? Wacko.'

'Drek!' Richie spat back, lemon juice squirting from his mouth. Then he seemed to spot something.

'Holy molé! Look who's walkin' this way.'

I looked. Like an answer to my prayers, two robed Spaniards were heading directly for us. Their robes were exactly the same kind as Bronzo and Bling were wearing; dark red, with a sort of white rope tied round the waist. They were hoodless, carrying their headgear under their arms.

Richie hopped along from one stall to the next, to keep up with us. 'Oh boy! This is your moment, kid. Your two lemonheads here have dug themselves a hole, and I'll bet they don't got the foggiest idea how to get out of it.'

He was right. I heard Bronzo whisper, 'Oh no, worra we going to do?'

'Take a chill pill, man!' insisted Bling.

'Yeah, but, d'you think they know, like?' said Bronzo.

'Just keep walkin', said Bling, 'an' leave the rest up to me, innit.'

The Spanish guys grinned as they approached us; it was clear that they believed Bronzo and Bling were their pals, other members of their brotherhood or whatever. They seemed quite young; one had a moustache, and the other had eyebrows that joined in the middle.

'Que pasa, amigos?' said the one with the moustache.

'Hola,' said Bling, at the ready with his best Spanish. He waved and slowed down, but didn't stop. The two others walked along with us; something I suspected Bling had not planned on.

'Hola,' copied Bronzo. Then silence. It was clear that the only Spanish Bronzo knew was words like 'bocadillo' that he picked up at the supermarket, and there was no need to discuss bread rolls right now.

As for Bling, my guess was that he knew more than Bronzo, but still not very much. I kept quiet. It would be so easy right now to point the finger, but so much better to let them incriminate themselves.

And it was fun watching them squirm.

The Spaniard with the monobrow peered through Bling's peepholes. 'Rodrigo?'

'No, amigo. Bl...B...uh, Bruno.'

The Spaniards looked at Bronzo, expecting a name from him as well.

Bronzo attempted to answer, but after saying, 'No, amigo, B...' he dried up, and Bling had to rescue him.

162

'Br…uh, Bruno,' said Bling again, unable to think of another vaguely Spanish-sounding name beginnning with 'B' that quickly.

'Se llama Bruno también?' said monobrow, raising it in surprise.

'Uh…si!' muttered Bling. Then, eager to escape the Spanish Inquisition, he patted el Moustachio on the arm, said, 'Adios, amigos!' and quickened his pace. But the Spaniards weren't to be shaken off that easily. They trotted alongside, and now el Moustachio was looking me up and down with intense interest. He was especially taken aback by the state of my feet.

'Quien es el niño?' he asked, nodding in my direction.

'Pedro,' said Bling.

El Moustachio reached across to shake my hand. 'Buenas tardes, Pedro!'

Obviously, neither Bronzo nor Bling wanted to let go of my hand, but el Moustachio still had his arm out, waiting, and no doubt he was growing more and more suspicious by the second. Bronzo held firm; he'd been told to leave everything up to Bling, so that was what he was doing. Bling held firm. He probably figured that since Bronzo was on my right, he might well let go at any moment, to free up my right hand to shake with. They were, of course, unable to signal to each other.

El Moustachio reached closer. 'Buenas tardes, Pedro!' he repeated. El Monobrow peered forward expectantly.

Bronzo and Bling hung on. Then the most fantastic, brilliant and amazing thing happened: they both let go at the same time.

I shot off into the crowds, weaving in and out; I was getting good at this. I came to the end of the avenue, where the stadium seating closed off in a big L-shape, and the crowds were applauding the procession as it drew nearer. *Parrum, parrum, parrum pom-pom*. I had no idea what was going on behind me, but I wasn't going to risk turning round, not for a nanosecond. For a moment, I thought I was going to be trapped, that the seating closed off the avenue, but as I got nearer I was relieved to see there was a way through. It took me into a square full of fountains, but the crowds were too thin here – I needed cover. I dashed across the square and then past a park, all luminous green in the city lights, then into a wide traffic-choked avenue. Gasping for breath, I got to the other side and allowed myself a glimpse back. A truck went by, then flash! A glimpse of red. They were crossing the road, no hoods now. It was them, no mistake; the broadness of Bling, the studded baldness of Bronzo. I had no idea if the Spaniards were behind, but I wasn't going to hang around to find out.

No side-street to turn down here; just railings, railings, but peering through them as I ran alongside I saw boats. Boats! I had reached the port. Up ahead, tall pillars that looked like an entrance; I bounded off in that direction, pavement stinging like jellyfish. I passed through the big gates, then wished I hadn't. This was even more wide open; a great vast motorway of a space, just some parked cars and the odd building here and there. No people, even. Oh, why did I have to come here? But perhaps by now I had shaken them off. For a moment, all I could hear was my own gasping breath. Maybe they didn't see me enter. Then came the footsteps and knew I wasn't safe yet.

I dived between a couple of parked cars. But this was the most brightly lit area of the port, and as I heard them draw nearer, I felt way too visible; I crept around the side of the car but how long could I go on dodging them like this? If I could just find something to hide *inside…*

Now the two of them split up; oh boy, there was no way one of them wouldn't nab me eventually! Sweating like crazy, I moved along the side of more vehicles until I was at the edge of the car parking area. If I were a cartoon right now, I'd be slinking round their bumpers, moulding myself to their forms…how great that would be! If only…

All that lay between me and the quayside was a large dark object; some sort of railtracks led up to it and now I saw it was a caboose, sitting with its couplings held out as if to greet me. Glancing back I saw that Bronzo and Bling were busy peering under cars: I headed for the caboose's embrace as fast as I could, thankful that my bare – if throbbing with pain – feet made hardly a sound.

I hid behind it, but this wouldn't provide cover for much longer; I must have been spotted, because here came those footsteps again. I glanced up at the big grey battleship moored beside me; no, that offered no place to hide. Then I saw what I had been praying for: a little boat. A tug boat, low enough for me to throw myself into; the perfect hiding place. Just in time, too; the footsteps were pounding nearer: *parrum, parrum, parrum pom-pom*. I ran to the edge of the quay and launched myself onto the boat; boof! My head collided with something hard and everything went dark.

Twenty-Four

Cold. Too much light. Reaching down for the covers, I found there weren't any. Wanted to get under something, wanted to be warm. Head hurt, wanted it to stop. Just sleep.

Sloop, sloop. Slopping, sucking noises. Wet, cold. Throbbing head. Snuggle down in this corner. Better. Need more sleep…

Later. *Sloop, sloop.* Even brighter; someone, please shut out the light! Warmer. Bright sun warming the breeze. Head heavy like a rock. Feet swollen. The two ends of me crying out in pain. I was rocking like a baby in a treetop, and sure enough, when I opened my eyes I saw just sky. But I wasn't up a tree, was I? Because I could feel hard floor under me. I pulled myself up and looked around. Over there, a tall white lighthouse. And in that direction, water, and a big grey battleship. Hey, that ship seemed familiar. Aha! The boat; yes, I was in fact on a boat. Strange, that. Then slowly, scenes from last night flashed up in my head like pieces of a jigsaw, and I began to put them into some sort of order. The parade, the chase, the two red-robed Spaniards; I wondered if they had caught Bronzo and Bling. Me jumping onto the boat. A tugboat by the looks of it, and right beside me an iron rail, which might well have had something to do with the whomping great bump that was throbbing away on my forehead like some sort of beacon. Never mind the lighthouse, boats coming into port could just follow Pablo's head.

Like the touch of a funny bone, I had a sense of something to be glad about: Hey! I'm free at last!

Then a second later, a heavy feeling: but still so far away from home. And very possibly Bronzo and Bling were still at large, tracking me down.

Hungry. I was very hungry. I thought of el Humptio handing me the money and dug into my pocket; yes, it was still there! Fantastic; I would go and have myself a slap-up breakfast somewhere. Then I would figure out what to do next. I dragged my creaking limbs out of the boat; I felt about a 102, and as if part of me were missing. It was a strange feeling, like I'd forgotten something; I even looked back into the boat. Ha! As if! Oops, mustn't forget my luggage, my backpack, my football kit.

The port was deserted; not surprising, really, since I guessed it was still quite early, and the whole town must have been up practically all night doing the

Good Friday boogie. Even the guard at the entrance to the port was having a snooze, his feet up in his little booth. I think I interrupted his dream, because after I passed by I heard him knock something over and swear in Spanish, then that loud, amplified air noise of a walkie-talkie.

I stepped cautiously out into the broad boulevard that had been so jammed with traffic the night before. Hardly anyone about now. In the emptiness I felt very conspicuous, and couldn't help clinging to cover, just in case. But I was *so* hungry, I just had to find something to eat.

I crossed the boulevard and headed up past the park with its tall palm trees until I came to a square by the cathedral, where a cafe was just opening up. A girl in a crisp black dress and even crispier white apron was setting up chairs and tables. Her glossy black hair was neatly scraped back off her face. I looked down at my shabby, definitely non-crisp self. My clothes looked as if I'd slept in them (probably because I had) and I was beginning to smell really rank. My feet looked as if they'd been up a chimney and back, and then there was the bump on my head which felt like one of those joke throbbing red jobs you get in cartoons, which magically disappear in the next scene. Only this one felt like it was planning to stick around for several days. Something told me she wasn't going to serve riff-raff like me. I gazed longingly at the pictures in the window of cold meat and cheese platters, till I noticed her staring daggers at me. She was very pretty. Hot-faced, I quickly looked the other way.

I went to the fountain in the middle of the square and splashed my face in the cool water, then cupped my hands and gulped it down, letting it spill all down my front. Then I wiped my face with my grubby T-shirt and moved on. As I went round the corner I tried to sneak another look at the girl, and walked straight into someone. My heart leapt, but it was just a baker delivering bocadillos. The rolls tumbled to the ground. I heard the girl's tinkling laugh echo around the square. 'Mires donde vais!' yelled the baker. This was all very familiar. It was just like that day Donald and I had been to the betting shop, when I first came face-to-face with L.J. The day my life went rotten. Boy, that felt like a lifetime ago! Several lifetimes, even; I felt like a cat who'd used up eight of its nine lives. A mangey old stray. The baker drove off in his truck, leaving the fallen bocadillos on the ground. I rescued three of them from the pigeons, and went and sat on the cathedral steps. The bread was deliciously warm, and chewy in the centre. I ate all three without stopping.

'So, you got away, huh? You showed 'em, those slimebucket pieces a drek! Good for you.'

Richie sat next to me on the step, eating crumbs and loudly smacking his lips, or whatever cockroaches have.

I looked at him in disgust. 'You're always eating!'

'Live to eat, eat to live, that's what I say. So, what's next on the me 'n' you, hey kid? You thought about it?'

'Well, you of all people should know you can't think on an empty stomach.'

'You're right there, kid. Good point. Still, you fixed that part, dincha? And you're free at last. Hey, with talents like yours, you could become famous! And what a place; the sun shines all year round, you could marry that cute Spanish waitress…'

I glared at him. 'Are you out of your mind? I'm going home! All I've got to do is find a phone. I've got some money…'

'Hey, if it's kidnappers you're worried about, you'd be rich enough to afford bodyguards!'

'You are really starting to annoy me,' I said, standing up. I headed down the steps and tried to concentrate on predicting my immediate future, like where I might find a public telephone.

Think, think…

'Huh! What a waste of freedom,' muttered Richie.

'Goodbye!' I snapped as I speeded up to try to get away from his irritating voice. *Think, think…*

I blinked hard. I shook my head. I slapped my temple: nothing.

Richie tumbled after me. 'What a waste of a brilliant talent!' he went on. 'So rare, so…'

I stopped and stared at him.

'Aha! Startin' to see some sense, huh?'

171

I just stood and stared.

'Kid, you're gettin' just a li-i-ittle bit spooky now. C'mon, out with it!'

'That's it!' I cried.

'That's what?'

'I've remembered what I've forgotten.'

'OK, now I'm thinkin' 'Funny Farm'. El Rancho del Crazios. What in the heck are you talkin' about?'

'When I woke up this morning, I knew something was missing. Now I know what it is. Richie, it's gone; I can't see the future any more.'

Twenty-Five

'You're serious?' said Richie, pure horror on his face.

'Yes, I'm serious. I just tried. It's gone.'

'Oh, no! You mean it just up and went? Where'd it go?'

'I don't know, maybe when I banged my head, or something…I knew I felt different.'

Richie began pacing up and down the step, waving his forelegs around. 'But that's terrible! It's a disaster!' He grabbed hold of my trouser-leg. 'You got anything else to eat? All this worrying's making me hungry!'

'No I haven't!'

He went back to pacing and wringing his hands, or whatever cockroaches have. Then he stopped.

'Hey! Maybe it's just temporary! Yeah, that's it. You just took a knock and jogged it, but maybe it'll come back in a while!'

I picked him up, his legs dangling. 'Richie, stop! Don't you see? I don't *want* it to come back; look at all the trouble it's caused me. I'm better off without it! Richie?'

Now Richie was staring into space. 'Are you playing some sort of game with me?'

Richie looked about as solemn as a cartoon cockroach can look. Which isn't very solemn, admittedly, but take it from me, he was deadly serious. 'No, kid. And speaking of forgetting, I think there's one very important thing you've forgotten. Do you hear that siren?'

There was a faint siren coming from somewhere. 'Er, yeah. So?'

'Ain't you forgettin' what those guys told you? About Antonio's police friend, and you being on their 'wanted' list?'

He was right; I had forgotten. But I just laughed. 'Ha! But nobody's going to want me any more, are they? I mean, since I've lost my clairvoyance, I'm not much use to L.J, or anyone else for that matter.'

'Wrong!'

'OK, so they don't know it yet, but once they do…'

The siren grew louder.

'Look, will ya do me a favour and hide, I'm gettin' nervous for you!'

'Why?'

Richie spoke very fast. 'Number one, the police at this point actually believe you stole that money from Antonio. Number two, you want my guess as to what'll happen when they bring you back? Antonio will suddenly discover that, 'Oh, that money wasn't stolen after all. My mistake, sorry to bother you."

'So that they'll hand me back, right?'

'Right. Because that was the object of the exercise; to get you back.'

'Yes, but when L.J finds out…'

'When L.J finds out you ain't no use to him any more…*cchhweeck*!' He made a throat-cutting action.

The siren wailed louder, and now everything in my poor, injured, muddled head made sense. That siren was for me. When Bronzo and Bling lost me in the port they were on the run themselves, from the two red-robed Spaniards, so they'd have cut right out of there. But they would have got a message to Antonio about where I'd last been seen, and Antonio or his sleazy police friend would have tipped off the Port Authority. For all I knew, they might even have gone round that night with torches; I was lucky they didn't find me. So when that sleepy old guard saw me – a bit late, but he did see me – he got straight onto the police. I was in more danger than ever; the boy who knew too much.

If they caught me, I was as good as dead.

Twenty-Six

Have you ever heard of doodlebugs? Yeah, they sound friendly, don't they? Little drawings of fun insects, cartoon cockroaches or whatever. Funny how the most terrifying things can have such cuddly names. My grandma's been dead a long time now, but I will never forget her story about the doodlebugs. It was wartime, and London was getting hammered by Hitler's forces. She never knew if her house would be the next one to be flattened, and the doodlebugs were the worst. They were pilotless planes carrying explosives. She would hear them flying over, *brr-r-r-r-r-rp*, but that wasn't the scary bit. Because as long as that engine was going, there was a chance it would pass you by; it was when the engine stopped that you had to worry. That was when it would drop out of the sky, and – *blam!* – you were blown to smithereens. That eery silence just before the explosion; those few seconds of terror, stayed with Grandma for the rest of her life.

That's how I felt when the siren stopped. It would have been different if it had faded away into the distance, but it didn't; it got louder and louder, then stopped. I ran down the cathedral steps, and across the street, but there wasn't time for me to hide. There was the piercing screech of a police whistle, and they were onto me.

I dashed up a narrow pedestrian street. Ahead was a small grocery shop, with a display of fruit and vegetables outside. Without thinking, I dived in under the crude table-and-crate arrangement, just managing to avoid colliding with a table leg and sending the whole caboodle crashing to the ground. It wasn't one of those set-ups like you see in London, all bright-green fake grass draped around. There was no cloth or anything to hide me, and as soon as I got under there I began to regret it. There was that police whistle again, coming closer. Beside me was an empty crate; moving at all was a gamble, but I weighed up the risk in my mind, and decided to take it. I pulled the crate toward me, then crouched down and pulled it over me. It was nowhere near big enough to hide me completely, but better than nothing. I sat with my chin between my knees, trying to stop myself from shaking, and – don't laugh – mentally apologising to the Virgin Mary. I should explain that this was because I was sitting on her at the time, or rather a poster with her face on it. I think the poster must have slipped from its spot on the window, and here it was underneath me. I'd seen the same one in practically every shop window in Malaga; a weddingey Mary with a white veil, fancy white-and-gold robe, and huge crown on her head framed with golden sun-rays. Her head tilted to one side, pearly tears riding down her cheeks. One of my weeping women! It reminded me of the Shed Drawings, and the other crying woman I'd drawn, the Picasso-ish one. And the casa, the house (with pigeons) and the baby. Woman, house, baby; the last three clues. Surely I could work out what they meant! Which woman, which house, which baby? Well, since I could no longer predict, I would need to rely on my wits alone to solve the riddle.

The policemen arrived at the shop and went in. Any moment now they would be coming out again, and if they looked under the fruit stand I was finished. I decided to take the risk and get out of there.

Making as little sound as possible, I climbed out from under my crate and made a dash to the corner of the street. As I turned the corner, I heard a voice cry out, 'Aqui estas!' I kept going, and now I got the spooky sensation they call *déjà vu*. You know, that feeling of 'I've been here before'? Hardly surprising, I hear you say, what with all the running away I'd been doing lately. You're probably experiencing a bit of *déjà vu* yourself by now, right? Bear with me, because this is where it gets seriously supernatural. I mean I *really* felt I'd been there before; right on this tiny, narrow street, with exactly these cobblestones with their squares-and-triangles pattern, and these houses crowding in either side with their shuttered windows and wrought iron balconies. The question racing through my mind as I ran and dodged the pedestrians, was: when?

There was commotion behind me, and there was that police whistle again. Oh yes, that had been in there too. When I was here before. And the fear, the terrible purple monster inside, making me want to cry out…

…But then I had cried out, hadn't I? All sorts of nonsense, but one thing was clear: casa. That's it! This was what I had dreamt the night of my fever; I had forgotten it all until this moment. What's more, I knew it had been a prediction, and that I would have to get somewhere; the casa. I remembered from the dream that there was a square…soon, soon, I would come to a square…

And then there was a square; big, open square. Big, open blue sky. Sky and trees…pigeons. Ah, yes! Pigeons…tall trees…tall monument. I ran to the monument, a big arrow pointing into the sky.

Weeyaw, weeyaw! Here was the police siren, coming from way over to my left…*peep! peep!* And here was the whistle coming from just behind me. Find the casa, and everything will be all right…I knew this from my dream, though I didn't know why; I was literally re-living it as each part unfolded. The casa was pulling me towards it, and as I ran I found myself drawn towards the far left corner of the square. Got to get to the far left corner…that was when the big hands grabbed me. *Flap flap flap!* went the pigeons, up in my face. Strong hands whisked my arms behind my back, and *clink!* went the handcuffs. The police car screeched to a halt nearby.

Then I heard my mother's voice cry out, 'Pablo!'

Twenty-Seven

Yes, it really was my mother. She had spotted me running across the square, from where she sat at a pavement café table at the corner of the square. The café was across the street from a building called the Casa Natal de Picasso. Do you know what that means? It's where Picasso was born. I learned that later, when things had calmed down.

Right now my mum was hugging me so hard I thought my eyes would pop out. And she *cried*; boy did she sob. I sobbed too. I couldn't hug her though, because I was still handcuffed. It was a moment before anyone realised that the policeman who had put the handcuffs on me had run off.

'Que intierro!' said his companion, and he ran off too. I was stuck there, my hands tied together, getting more confused by the minute. The other policemen, the ones who had just got out of the car, were yelling to each other in Spanish. Then one jumped back in the car and went screaming off again, while the other one stayed with us.

'Es tu Pablo Cchhobbs?' he asked me gutterally, sweat dribbling down his temples, with a very discombobulated look on his face.

'Yes, yes!' cried Mum. 'He's here! My boy! We've found him at last! Oh, my boy, my lovely boy…'

* * *

So there you have it: I was right, she'd read the signs.

Woman crying = probably represents herself, but let's not forget the Picasso-ishness; big clue.

House = Casa Natal.

Baby = the infant Pablo Picasso.

Another clue that I didn't get because I didn't have the drawings in front of me: the baby, when I saw it again, did look a lot like Picasso. Big black, staring eyes. She'd picked up on that, my mum. And then there were the pigeons; she showed me how one of them looked exactly like a print Picasso had made, called the 'dove of peace'. I'd never seen it before; it wasn't even in that book I'd read about him. But I'd drawn it.

There were other things I could have kicked myself about; apparently it said in the book that he was born in Malaga, but I probably never read that part. Because to be honest, when I say I *read* that book, I mean I looked at the pictures and read little bite-size chunks of it here and there. Mostly stuff about when he was a boy, getting into trouble, hanging out with the gypsies and really cool stuff like that. Not, you know, he was born here, he painted that painting in that year, blah, blah, all the boring guff. The juicy bits.

Anyway, you can see how Mum managed to put together all these pieces of the puzzle, once Donald had shown her my drawings and explained that they were predictions (which, as I had expected, was exactly what happened). They led her to what she would call an 'inescapable' conclusion: that she would find me in Malaga, at the Casa Natal. She even knew about the Spanish Holy Week stuff, recognized that that was what my 'ghosts' and 'funeral' were all about. So she guessed that she would find me before the week was up. Amazing, huh? She's a dark horse, my mum; I never thought of her as especially clever till now. I think she even surprised herself. She'd shown my drawings to the English police, of course. But they wouldn't treat them as evidence, so although they were searching for me, she was on her own with that particular line of enquiry.

You want to know who that policeman was, who caught me, then ran away? Yeah, you probably guessed it; Antonio's friend. There he was, thinking he'd got me at last and was *this* close to that fat juicy wad of cash from Antonio. But as soon as it became clear that the woman rushing towards us crying, 'Pablo!' was one desperate mum, about to be reunited with her son, he realised he was in big trouble. He sure as hell wasn't going to stick around to answer any awkward questions about why he was trying to arrest me. They got him, by the way; we saw the weasel-face at the police station, hanging his head in shame.

As Ruiz, the one who rescued me put it, 'What is it they say in American films? We sniff the rat.'

'Smell a rat,' I corrected.

'Were you with two men, pretending they were Spanish and wearing the robes for Semana Santa?'

'Yes! Bronzo and Bling.'

('Ohh!' went Mum, chewing her knuckles.)

I rubbed her back. 'I got away though,' I added.

'I know this,' said Ruiz. 'We had a report last night, somebody saw you…'

'El Moustachio and El Monobrow!' I exclaimed.

Ruiz frowned at me. 'Eh?'

'I mean, the guys from the parade.'

'That's right. It seems they nearly caught this – what did you say their names were, Bob and Bing?'

'Bronzo and Bling.'

Ruiz jotted this down, muttering, 'These are not their real names, I think?'

I shrugged. 'I never heard them called anything else.'

'We have been looking for these bad men since last night,' Ruiz continued. 'They were last seen chasing you towards the port, so we sent out a radio message. That guy' – he jabbed his pen in the direction of weasel-face – 'he must have recognized the description of the men; he responded immediately, saying he and his colleague were down near the port and would search for them.'

'...Except he was only interested in tracking *me* down...'

'Mmm-hmm,' said Ruiz, tapping his pen on the table in barely-contained anger. '*And* stopping anyone else from arresting Bonzo and Bring, don't forget...He arrested two guys, but later he let them go. "Mistaken identity," he said. Pah! The trouble-crosser!'

'Double-crosser,' I corrected again. 'I missed all that; must have been after I passed out.'

'You passed out? Oh, my poor love!' whimpered Mum.

'Where were you?' asked Ruiz. 'Nobody could find you.'

'I was at the port, in a tug-boat...' Piecing it all together, it seemed that the port official who'd spotted me that morning must have reported it to weasel-face – at his instruction, no doubt – which was how he and his friend got on my trail.

'You scum!' Mum spat out at weasel-face, really loud.

'Mum!' I nearly fell over; I'd never heard her so passionate in my entire life.

'Was only this morning I discovered he wasn't even stationed down by the port – that's when we got suspicious and decided to find out what he was up to.'

So: one down, four to go. How were we going to catch L.J, and the rest of them? Simple: we get weasel-face to lead us to them. But, as Ruiz put it, 'we don't have much time. We must be putting up the tail…'

'…Hightail it…'

'Yes, cchh-ightail it. We think they are already in hiding.' He turned to the other officers who were holding weasel-face. 'Bien, vamos!'

Twenty-Eight

One Year Later:

I'm sitting on top of the world. Or a pile of poo, depending on how you look at it. Whatever, it's a big ball made from recycled tyres, and if you put it in my bedroom, it would fill it all up except for the corners. Next to it is a giant beetle, looks a bit like Richie Roach. It's a scuplture, and – you're not going to believe this – it was made by my mum and dad. And guess what? It's fantastic! It's called Recycling Richie, and I worked on it too, as Kid Consultant. Because this isn't just any old sculpture, it's one that you can climb on. You can get inside the ball and run in it, like a hamster. And as you do you get daylight, darkness, daylight, darkness, where parts are solid rubber and others are all holey. The beetle's not exactly like the one you see on TV, but then we didn't want it to be. It's more just inspired by him, like instead of being brown, this one's just wild and wacky in different colours, all recycled stuff but not ugly like you'd think that would be. Beautiful reds and greens, oranges and yellows from old cans dipped in some sort of resin to protect them from the elements. The maddest, fabbest, beetle you ever saw.

It's been a mad, fab time. Although if you drew a chart of ups and downs, starting from when we arrived back in England, it would look like this:

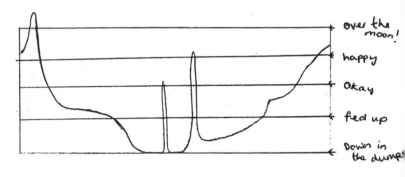

over the moon!

happy

Okay

fed up

Down in the dumps!

As you can see, there was a really high bit right at the beginning – that was getting the news that L.J, Bronzo and Bling had been caught, and were being brought back to England to stand trial. That was mega-brilliant, I can tell you. Practically dancing on the rooftops, we were. Then a dip: I was big news. They interviewed me for the national newspapers, I was on the 10 o'clock news and everything. So was Mum (Dad stayed out of it). I didn't mind at first, and I guess I needed to talk about it. But I wasn't prepared for how much everyone was really into my story, wanting to know more, and more, and after a while I just wanted them all to go away. I wanted everything to be normal. Eventually Mum put her foot down and said, 'No more; leave us alone to get on with our lives.' The phone went on ringing for a while, but pretty soon we were old news anyway, so they went on to the next thing.

See that little blip, right around then? That was Mum going out and buying a second-hand TV, without consulting Dad. I thought that was a bit brilliant of her. Mind you, I don't think she was only thinking of me; I heard her talking to Aunt Dot on the phone the other day, and she was saying, 'You were absolutely right, he hardly ever watches it now. He wasn't even bothered when I cancelled the cable connection...yes, it was a good move.'

I suppose it's true; you always want what you can't have. It was great to start with though, and it's still really excellent to be able to watch the football. But I'm less interested in watching cartoons now than drawing and writing them myself. I do it every chance I get; I've invented loads of characters.

There's another blip right after that one. That's my mum and – *bing!* – lightbulb going on over her head.

Big idea.

Twenty-Nine

Mum's big idea happened when we were watching Richie Roach together (amazing, huh? She wanted to see it for herself, you see). Anyway, Richie was rolling together a big ball of buttery toast crumbs, and Mum goes, 'He looks like a scarab.'

So I said, 'What's a scarab?'

She gave me an affectionate dig in the ribs. 'You know, the dung beetle.'

'Oh, is that the one that rolls up balls of cow poo?'

'Yes, just like he's doing with those crumbs. The ancient Egyptians worshipped the scarab beetle.'

'Oh yeah, I remember learning about that. Ha!' I laughed, watching Richie get stuck in a blob of marmalade. 'I knew that was going to happen!' Then the commercials came on. 'Fancy worshipping a beetle,' I said on my way to the biscuit tin. ''Specially one that spends its whole time mucking about with poo.'

'Well, you know why,' said Mum, as she began rifling through the enormous mound of newspapers on the coffee table.

'I just remember something about a giant beetle rolling the sun across the sky,' I said, munching a Hob-Nob.

'Yes, that's how they saw their sun-god. The scarab was thought to be immortal, because it lays its eggs in the dung ball...Why does your father never throw his newspapers away? This one's three weeks old! Where's today's?' She began flinging papers all over the place.

I sat down with the biscuit tin. 'You were saying.'

Mum looked up, frowning. 'What?'

'About the beetle eggs.'

'Oh yes, well, the point is, the Egyptians weren't aware of the egg-laying; they just observed the newly-hatched beetles appearing miraculously from the dung. So the dung beetle became a god of creation. Do you know what, I'm going to have a massive clearout. I'm sick of looking at this lot.' She kicked at a dusty old pile of art journals. 'He hasn't even picked one of these up since about 1987. Ugh!'

'Not now Mum, look; Richie's coming back on.'

'Sheesh!' went Richie, trying to pull his feet out of the orange goo. 'All a guy wants to do is clean a plate, an' this happens! I coulda sworn this was a Jelly-Free Zone.' SPLOTCH! goes another blob of marmalade, and now he realises he's being bombarded by Gladiator and his Marmalade CATapult TM.

Help!

Well, he gets out of it, of course; by going into 'super-suction' mode. Meanwhile, Mum started going into a super-suction mode of her own, cramming old newspapers and magazines into bags. She filled a supermarket bag so full, it broke and everything splurged all over the floor. 'Oh damn!'

I went to help. It's funny, I thought; none of this stuff used to bother her. But suddenly, seeing the steely determination with which she shook out a new bag and started all over again, I saw that 'starting again' was what it was all about; clean slate. My kidnap had been a wake-up call, and suddenly she needed to see life B.K. (before the kidnap) as a closed chapter; there was no looking back, only going forwards.

'...And you know what I'm going to do next?' she went on, getting shriller by the moment. 'Get that whole backyard sorted out. I'm sick of it!' she said. 'Oh, why can't your father be more like...like...'

'Richie Roach?' I suggested. 'He's *always* cleaning up. Look how he got out of that mess with the marmalade.'

Mum laughed. (That's right, she laughed; she hardly ever used to.) 'Exactly!' she added. 'Three cheers for Richie Roach, he should win an award. Let's build him a monument.' Then she stood bolt upright and blinked. 'Pabs!' (She never used to call me 'Pabs'!)

'What?'

'That's what I'm going do! I'm going to make a sculpture in honour of that much-maligned creature, the glorious cockroach! A scarab beetle for our times, if ever there was one!'

'You don't do sculpture,' I said.

She flung the bag of newspapers into the corner. 'No, that's right, I don't! Just like you never used to draw – now there's no stopping you! So who's to say I can't start?'

I grinned at her. She reminded me of something – myself, when I first discovered cartoons. 'Would it be a big sculpture?' I asked.

'Hu-mungous!' said Mum, spreading her arms.

'Hey, I've got another idea,' I said. 'Remember that exhibition we went to years ago when I was little, when I got upset because I wasn't allowed to climb on the sculptures?'

'Do I ever!' said Mum. 'You brought the house down.'

I remembered it vividly. I couldn't understand why Dad held me back, and in the end we had to leave, I was yelling my head off and people were staring and tut-tutting. There had been one sculpture in particular; it was so inviting, carved out of milky-white stone, all rounded with a Pablo-sized hole in it. I just wanted to be inside it; it seemed to me as if that was what it was made for.

193

'Well,' I said, 'why not make a sculpture that kids are *meant* to climb on?'

'Oh, yes!' cried Mum. 'Why stop at one, for that matter? Why not have a whole park full of interactive sculptures?'

'Yeah! And no snotty guards shooing you away. Fantastic!'

'Brilliant,' said Mum. 'Pablo, I'm going to find us a location for this project and when I do, you're going to be Kid Consultant…oh, I've had it with this stuff!' She tugged at one of the zip-lock bags on her 'Bits of Dead People' collection. She pulled it off the big white canvas and chucked it on the floor. She pulled off another, and another. 'I hate it! It's so dull; I mean really, why should anyone care?'

'Can I help?' I asked.

'Yes! Yes! Down with death, up with life! Hurray!'

'Hurray!' I joined in, and now the two of us were hurling the bags of dead bits all around the room, laughing.

'What on earth…' said Dad, appearing at the back door.

'Down with death!' screeched Mum, throwing a bag. It hit the lampshade, sending out a cascade of dust.

'Up with life!' I added, bouncing on the couch and throwing up a considerably larger dust-cloud.

Dad grimaced. He caught sight of the bagged-up art journals. 'My journals…what are they doing in there?'

'Recycling!' said Mum. 'Out with the old, in with the new. Listen, we've had the most brilliant idea!' She went over and grabbed him by his moth-eaten cardigan sleeves. 'We can work on it together, all three of us!'

Dad looked at her as if she'd gone mad, then turned to me. 'What's going on?' he asked, looking bemused. 'Wenda, will you just calm down and tell me what this is all about?'

'Beetles!' she proclaimed grandly. 'Cockroaches!' Then she collapsed on the couch in a fit of giggles, and that set me off as well.

Dad was not amused. 'Wenda, I don't know what's got into you, but—'

Mum stood up. 'I'll tell you what's got into me!' she cried, suddenly very serious. 'Real life's got into me! Oh Humphrey, don't you see? Everything's changed. For heaven's sake, we nearly lost our son! I want to celebrate life, not go on about death all the time. It's so dull and depressing!'

Dad folded his arms. 'Oh, so now you want to be an entertainer, is that it?' The word 'entertainer' couldn't have been uttered with more disgust.

Something inside me snapped. 'No, that's not what she means!' I yelled. 'I know exactly how Mum feels. It was the same for me when I discovered cartoons. And you…well, you'd better sit up and take notice, or—'

I was shaking. Mum touched me on the shoulder, silencing me. 'A sculpture park, Humphrey,' she said softly, her eyes glassy with tears. 'Think how fantastic that could be!'

Dad stared at us both. 'Huh!' he said at last. 'And where's the money going to come from eh? It's all very well having these grandiose ideas, but we'd never get anyone to pay for the thing.'

'Oh won't we?' challenged Mum, putting her arm around me. 'Well you're forgetting one thing.'

And suddenly I understood what she meant. 'Yeah, Dad,' I added. 'We're famous!'

Mum went over to the telephone and dialled.

Thirty

It took a while before Mum persuaded Dad to get involved. But once he did, there was no looking back. If he's happy, well he's not exactly leaping about and yelling it from the roof-tops, but then that's not Dad's way, and it never will be. But he's loosened up, no doubt about that.

As for Aunt Dot, well, we hardly ever see her now. She's gone to live in Devon with Ned Komm, a bearded furniture restorer. She's still painting dots. She hasn't married him yet, but I like the idea that if she does, she could become Dot Komm.

* * *

Anyway, about those cartoons I'd been drawing: I invented two new characters the other day, Pig and Casso. Casso's a boy superhero, rescuing people all over the world in typical superhero fashion, except he can't fly. So he rides on the back of Pig, a pig (who can).

197

One day, Casso's doorbell rings, and two guys are standing there with a package. 'Yo. Delivery, man,' says the big one.

'Jist sign here, like,' says the other one, handing Casso a form and a pen. Casso signs, brings in the mystery package and opens it up. It is a very cute, live pink bunny.

Pig goes, 'Don't look at it, it's a trick!'

But it is too late; Casso has looked into its eyes and — cue whirly-squirly eye-effect — he is under its spell. He gets a call for an emergency, but instead of going to the rescue aboard Pig, he says, 'I'm gonna stay right here and play with this cutesy-wutesy bun-bunn.'

'C'mon kid, don'tcha know who sent you that rabbit?' says Pig. 'Only your arch enemy. the evil El Jay, who's bent on world domination.'

'Oh, never mind,' says Casso. 'Hey little bunny, let me find you a yummy carrot.'

'But kid, there's no time to lose! I can't do this by myself!'

'...Maybe a nice lettuce leaf. Oh, you are a lovely bunny-wun!'

Then Pig takes another emergency call; guards at Fort Knox are wandering off, lured by cute little pink bunnies. 'Oh no!' says Pig. 'El Jay's planning a raid!'

Pig does everything in his power to distract

Casso, from trying to destroy the bunny to attempting to get Casso on his back so he can fly him off. Everything fails. Finally he hits on an idea; he persuades Casso that little bunnsy might really love to see him in his superhero outfit.

'Yeah!' says Casso. 'I think ickle wabbit might weally like that!'

So he puts it on, x-ray specs and all, and SHOCK! HORROR! With the specs he is able to see the furry bunny for what it really is: A HORRIBLE, EVIL MONSTER! Quick as a flash, he destroys the monster and he's on the back of Pig, flying to rescue the nation's riches from the clutches of the evil El Jay. Pig and Casso save the day once again!

The End

You probably recognised some characters in there. And maybe you figured that Casso is me - or an American me, at any rate. Then there's the 'gift', and what a terrible gift! But one that seemed so great at first. Where did it come from? I called it a gift from the devil, but that just makes me think of some red-faced guy with horns and a pitchfork ruling the Underworld, and then I get the giggles. Anyway what's the diff; thinking about where my gift came from and where it went to is all just missing the point, I reckon.

In any case, the more I think about it, the more I think it was just my juice box overflowing. See, say you've got, I don't know – a garden hose. And you just let the water trickle out happily, going with the flow. Well, it responds to gravity, doesn't it? Just pours. But if you put the tap on full blast, but close off the hose squirter thingy, then the pressure builds up and builds up, so that when you finally let it go, it goes *whoosh!* this way and that – all over the place. I reckon it was the same with me and my cartoons; even before I knew it, some impulse was growing and growing inside me all those years; that little creative spark that I didn't have the chance to connect to, because…well, I guess because I don't respond to gravity…the *seriousness* kind, that is. Or all that pressure. So when that valve was finally opened, it splurged so far, it raced off into the future.

Er, or something like that.

Oh, I don't know! Who ever knows where any ideas comes from? One thing's for sure; my 'Pig and Casso' cartoon story tells you just how I feel about my gift now; even if it ever had the chance of being any good to anyone, it was a dangerous thing to have, and I'm glad to be shot of it.

Anyway, I'm off to the Post Office now with this; I'm entering 'Pig and Casso' for an animation competition. First Prize: your cartoon gets made.

Fingers crossed.

Acknowledgments

Once again, many thanks to my cousin Mat for all his help with the police stuff, and to Lee Weatherly for her valuable opinion. Thanks to Pamella Weekes for her help with the Spanish. And again I thank my husband Pano for indulging my whims, even when there was no prospect of a publishing contract in sight.